BURNING RUBBISH

Travel, Terrorism & Life

By R. J. BRENNAN

https://www.rjbrennan.com.au

Instagram.com/burning_rubbish

Paperback – 978-0-6459108-0-3

eBook – 978-0-6459108-1-0

PREFACE

This book is a work of fiction inspired by true events.
Some of the stories told herein have only been possible
to depict in such detail through the author's experiences
serving with the Australian Defence Force, its Allies,
and partners.

The author has changed the times, dates, and names due
to classification or operational importance. This book is
not an accurate description of history; however, the
experiences and emotions are real. Any resemblance
to real persons living or dead is purely coincidental.

Many people have contributed to the making of this book,
and without them, the characters would not have come to
life. The author is forever grateful for the mark they have
left on his life and this story.

The author would also like to acknowledge the first
responders and medical staff who saved countless lives
during the events covered in this book and continue to
do so.

Those involved with the writing of this book pay their
deepest respect to the families of those who were killed
in action.

Lest we forget.

PROLOGUE

Derrick burst to life at the sound of the base alarm and struggled to put on his helmet and body armour while still in bed. He grabbed his rifle as he left his room, and then ran through a lane of reinforced T-walls to a bunker, where he dropped to his knees in the dirt. His heartbeat pounded through his eardrums, and he slowed his breathing to regain composure. *Incoming—incoming—incoming* rang out across the public address system and Derrick's radio crackled to life.

"Theatre ballistic missiles inbound," said a soldier from the Operations Centre.

"More to follow, wait out."

Soldiers and civilians lined the walls of the bunker and Derrick stared at the silhouettes around him, all waiting for impact.

He often thought of his parents escape from Iran when he sat in hardened bunkers listening to landing rockets that the Militia had fired at them. For so long he'd resented his parents and their adventures … he would never live up to the bar they had set.

But the monkey on his back was the same old foe, and he'd never admit it was them who led him out of the doldrums of youth.

Well, here I am Geoff … At war with your old mates …

The ground shuddered and a dull rumble felt like rounds were slowly creeping towards them. Everybody sat still and listened intently.

His father, Geoff, had worked for a U.S. military contractor, and his mother, Kate, worked for the British Embassy in Tehran.

At the time his parents were there, the Shah was the Monarch, and his policies of westernisation, modernisation and secularisation created vast amounts of money for foreign contractors, who flocked to the country in droves. Iranian opposition to the West increased, and those who stood to gain from the Shah's policies ended up in the peoples' crosshairs.

The student protest movement was fanatic, and speakers on rooftops broadcast "down with the Shah" and "remove the USA" across the city.

Derrick recalled his mother's story, pretty much word-for-word, of how she and her colleague Maree had walked headfirst into the resentment of Westerners when thousands of demonstrators blocked their way to work one morning. Scared witless, they bashed on the window of an antique store that hadn't opened for trade that day.

"Help, let us in!" they screamed, white with fear. A man in white robes opened the front door and stared at them both.

"Yalla," he said as he hurried them into the darkness of the shop and gestured to them to get behind a bookshelf. They held their breath and wept as the mob went by, while the smell of musty and stale air strangled their sobs.

Kate had told him that she and Maree formed quite a friendship working at the Embassy, and they'd found comfort in each other, having both followed their husbands to a foreign land. When the demonstrators passed, they pulled over their head scarfs and held hands before quietly leaving the shop.

The morning after the demonstration Maree failed to show at work, and a week later Kate still knew nothing of her whereabouts. When Maree didn't turn up the following Monday, Kate threw herself into the Ambassador's office in tears.

"Where is Maree?" she yelled. "What's happened to her?"

The Ambassador's aide quickly put her arms around Kate and walked her outside the office.

"She's under house arrest," said the staff officer quietly.

"What does that mean?" asked Kate, inconsolable.

"Her husband has asked that she stay home and not return to work," said the staffer. "The authorities might jail her if she does."

Kate felt sick, worried and helpless.

The authorities had put a curfew in place where citizens of Tehran were not to be on the streets from dusk until dawn, and Maree's husband had taken the warning a step too far. Kate arrived home that afternoon and a knock at the door sent her to her knees.

"Who is it?" asked Kate, shivering and in tears.

"I'll check," said Geoff, hurriedly walking down the stairs.

Kate heard yelling in Persian and footsteps entering the house. She fainted from fear and when she woke, she found a couple in their twenties escaping the curfew and drinking tea with Geoff.

From then on, Kate dreaded leaving the house and simple tasks like going to the butcher became embarrassing and enraging. She always dressed modestly and would wait politely to order.

"May I have some beef?" asked Kate one day at the butcher shop down the road from their house. She stood in the shadow of dead carcasses where the butcher continued to serve others. Only when she was the last person in the shop, did the butcher turn to her and smile.

"Please, we pray," he said before turning his back and leaving the room.

Lamb skulls stared at Kate as she waited a few minutes before the butcher returned.

"Go away, we are closed," the butcher shouted, incensed she was still there. His eyes pierced through Kate as he pointed her out of the shop.

Desolate, Kate left and returned home, where Geoff was counting money on the bed. "They hate us here Geoff and I understand why," she said. "We need to leave."

The next morning, armed guards intercepted Kate before she could enter the Embassy, where a group of protesters had begun to mingle. The guards told her that the U.S. was evacuating all personnel to the UK and that she would be on her own if she decided to stay. Helicopters circled above and the armed guards moved her through the crowd inside the building. She got to her desk and picked up the handset on her telephone before winding the dial to call Geoff at work.

"Geoff, we're leaving," said Kate with panic in her voice. "We're being evacuated from the Embassy — you can meet us at the air base."

"Shit, what about our things?" Geoff responded, angry at the lack of warning.

"Leave everything and get to the air base," said Kate. "Money's worthless if we're dead."

"Look … You get to London, and I'll make my own way back," said Geoff.

"Geoff, I have to go," cried Kate, against the calm but nonetheless frantic sounds of an evacuation in full swing. "They want us to move to aircraft on the roof. I'll be at your parents' place in London if I don't see you."

Guards then moved Kate to the roof where two helicopters had rotors turning. They marshalled her on board, and within a matter of seconds, she was high above Tehran and bound for the UK.

AH-64 Apache Air Weapons Teams flew over Camp Cooke, which focused Derrick's attention to the present as more radio traffic was heard over the net.

"AWT's airborne and moving to overwatch. Theatre Ballistic Missiles two minutes to impact."

If the Militia exploit the missile strike at least the Apaches are on station thought Derrick as he was drawn back to thoughts of his parents' escape.

In his office across from Mehrabad air base in '79, Geoff, who was usually calm in the face of danger, screamed, "Shit!" as he watched the helicopters take-off and land.

They must be from the Embassy.

It crossed his mind to race over, but he didn't want to just up and leave, or break his lucrative contract. His American boss heard him shout and came out from his office to see what was going on.

"What's happening, Amigo?" said the American.

"Kate's just been bloody evacuated from the Embassy," said Geoff.

"You're not thinking of leaving too, are you?"

"No," said Geoff. "I'll see if thing's quieten down a bit … I'm just worried about Kate, that's all."

"Why don't you move closer to work … if it does get worse it'll be easier to leave. There's still money to be made here Geoff, lots of it," said the American with his hands on his hips staring out at the base.

Geoff left work and arrived home, where a group of neighbours stood outside menacingly.

"Why are you in this country?" said one of the neighbours. "Leave Iran and go home!"

"I'll be gone today," replied Geoff solemnly as he entered the house.

It wasn't a good time to be a Westerner in Tehran, resentment gripped the populace and Geoff felt tension everywhere.

"I'm sorry, we don't have room," said the hotel manager upon Geoff's arrival at a hotel close to the air base.

"Please, I have nowhere to stay," replied Geoff.

"The mob will kill both of us if they find out you stay here," the manager went on.

"I beg you, I have nowhere else." The hotel manager stared through him before reluctantly handing over a key.

"Down the hall on the left," said the manager.

In his small room, Geoff turned on the TV. The news reported a million people marching from central Tehran to Modern Arch, which was close to the hotel. The crowds chanted: "Death to the Shah. Death to the Shah and his family!" Banks, cinemas and anything that symbolised the West were set alight.

Geoff sat on the end of the bed and watched intently before a loud thump on his door made the blood drain from his face.

"Sir, please, you have to leave," said the hotel manager nervously. "Many people are coming, and they will hang you in the street."

Geoff collected his bags, and the manager helped him to the hotel basement where a taxi was waiting. Knowing his time in Iran had just ended he looked at the driver, "To the air base please," he said.

"Lie down," the driver replied.

Quickly, Geoff lay down on the back seat and the driver threw a blanket over the top of him while the manager shoved his bags in the boot.

Chanting crowds had begun to fill the streets in anticipation of the march, but the driver sped through them to the air base and in a matter of minutes with his life still intact Geoff arrived at the air base.

After giving his driver the last of his ill-gotten gains, Geoff walked to British Embassy staff who'd established an evacuee handling centre near the front gate.

"You should have left with Kate," said an angry staff officer when she looked at his passport. But before Geoff got the right of reply, armed security directed him to a RAF Hercules bound for Cyprus.

Goeff left Iran, Ayatollah Khomeini took control of the country and the Shah fled to America. Two years later, in 1982, Derrick was born in London, where soft rock blasted from cassette players across the country.

Now as Derrick hummed 'Come on Eileen', torchlight flickered through the bunker and deep thuds in the distance made dust fall from the roof like snow.

In a case of history repeating, like his parents before, Derrick sat in Iranian cross hairs as the Islamic Republic tried to purge Westerners from the Middle East.

Come on ya bastards! Get it over with ...

CHAPTER 1

Derrick wasn't much of a student despite his parents' education and travel, and he left high school at fifteen to work at the shipping wharfs in Sydney. His boss was a leathery old bloke with a rum cigar permanently attached to his bottom lip, who continually rotated though the same handful of tales from his youth.

"Back in my day, I had to fight the boss for me wage … you blokes get it too easy," he told Derrick each pay Friday.

Derrick lived with his mate Dingo at the beach in a two-bedroom apartment known as the Rat Pack. Dingo was a south coast hippy, and the pair raced home each day to surf and chase girls under a warm blanket of booze and dope. However, real-world problems began to encroach on their sheltered youth, and politics and ignorance landed at their doorstep.

Middle Eastern gangs had hit the headlines, and racist commentary burnt white-hot throughout the media. Images of drunk white Australian kids with, "we grew here, you flew here," on their t-shirts depicted Australia as a continent full of ignorant convicts. Teenagers and violent criminals were dividing multicultural Australia.

Derrick and Dingo had been surfing when a text message went viral.

Every fucking Aussie get to the beach and take back our pride — this shit is on it read. The boys returned to the Rat Pack just as a crowd began to build in the sandy streets.

"Dezza, what the fuck is going on? My phone is off the hook!" Dingo laughed.

"One of the boys just said get down to the park," replied Derrick. "Apparently some dude and his girl just got beat up on the beach. Dickheads from out of town, no doubt."

Derick and Dingo grabbed some beers and split up to meet their mates in a crowded park where some 'blow-ins' were causing trouble. A ring of people circled the thugs and Derrick watched on from a distance.

"You want a fucken go?" screamed one of the thugs as he locked eyes on his target.

"Look man, I don't want any trouble," said Dingo with his hands high in the air.

Wild with adrenaline, and committed to fight-not-flight, the shirtless attacker ran at Dingo and delivered a powerful right cross to his face. The crowd dispersed like a bomb had dropped and Dingo was left unconscious in the crater. Two unknown girls raced over to nurse him, and the sound of sirens forced the thugs to flee. Dingo limped to a waiting ambulance with a girl under each arm and blood streaming from his nose.

"Have you got their numbers?" laughed Derrick, who was briefing the paramedics. Dingo gave a toothless smile, then got in the van with the girls and closed the door. Police arrested the gang, who were hiding in the pub, where they were mocked mercilessly for their stupidity.

The local pub was a rite of passage and most of Derrick and Dingo's mates had lifetime bans. It was a typical beach-side scene where the locals hated the bouncers, and the feeling was reciprocated.

Derrick's mate Moose and his rivalry with mutant bouncer the Octopus was one of the great match-ups of local pub warfare. Moose was a strapping young fella, Scandinavian in appearance and Viking-like in build.

The Octopus was a thickset, dreadlocked bouncer whose knockouts were as legendary as his hatred for locals. He loathed Moose and ejected him at every opportunity. Moose generally avoided his gaze until it was dark and he was eight beers deep and feeling confident.

"Oi, cockhead," shouted Moose one evening.

The Octopus and his right-hand man looked over. Derrick and a group of his mates had joined two tables together and were smoking cigarettes on the terrace. Beer glasses littered the table and screams of laughter contrasted against the thud of bad music from the millennium.

The bouncers walked over and warned them to behave.

"The boys are looking for trouble again, ey?" said the Octopus in a Kiwi accent.

Moose's girlfriend Sharon tried to pacify the moment. "We're not doing anything wrong. Leave us the fuck alone."

"Oh, hang on a minute," said Moose. "Bob Marley just called; he said he wants his hair back."

The table erupted with laughter and the bouncers swooped in and manhandled Moose into the street, where the crowd looked on and cheered.

Once freed, Moose's eyes turned from blue to red and he turned around to level the score. The situation quickly turned into a brawl and he and Sharon legged it home.

The next day, Moose's portrait hung like the Queen's at the entrance to the pub with the post nominal: not welcome.

It wasn't always booze and fights when the surf was flat, and Derrick and his mates hunted fish through the kelp, getting spooked by shadows cast by clouds. Occasionally they saw sharks, but none gave them a real scare.

When there were waves, Derrick and his mates went to the Royal National Park to trek down a goat track to an isolated beach. The track descended an escarpment and snaked through a temperate rainforest that led to a grass plateau, which gently rolled onto the beach below. Surf shacks built during the Great Depression of the 1930s blended into the landscape at the shoreline.

Dingo was mates with a bloke whose shack had been passed down through his family, and the mate asked him to renovate the place before it turned into dust. The owner had little money, but offered to pay him with the weed he grew in the tundra.

"Resilient plant, this one," said the owner. "What do you say?"

"Fuck yeah," Dingo replied, and he returned from work each afternoon with a new batch that he smoked with Derrick on the balcony of the Rat Pack. They compared the effects of bush smoke versus hydroponic and played the guitar until they drifted off to sleep on the couch.

Derrick's dad Geoff hated Dingo and he cornered him at a BBQ just before Derrick was about to go overseas.

"Dingo, I know blokes like you," said Geoff. "You drink, you smoke dope and you're reckless. You corrupt people and bring them down to your level in life. I don't want you influencing my son."

"Fuck off, Geoff." Dingo retorted. "Who do you think you are?"

If anyone was doing the corrupting it was Derrick — who was enjoying life to the fullest, and Geoff and Kate were simply in the way.

CHAPTER 2

At nineteen, Derrick flew to Canada to escape his parents' clutches. Sick of the family bullshit, he wanted to hit the eject button. With a couple of thousand dollars, he grabbed his backpack, put a snowboard under his arm and took himself to the airport. Twenty hours later he arrived in Vancouver, where the smell of cinnamon doughnuts and filtered coffee welcomed him.

It was early in the morning, and airport staff had just started the breakfast in the arrivals' hall.

"Try one of the Beaver tails, Sir," offered a woman, pouring coffee as Derrick collected his snowboard.

I've only been here two minutes, and they want me to eat their national animal for fuck's sake.

He politely declined before collecting his bag and snowboard on his way to the Greyhound bus bound for Whistler.

He stayed with a couple of blokes from Melbourne in a small but lively hostel, where they drank beer, went to parties and ripped up the mountain each day.

One frosty morning, Derrick caught an edge on his board going down a tree line and speared headfirst into snow which was, in fact, the entrance to a cave. Apparently, all that could be seen from behind was Derrick's board — and the two lads pulled him out before a black bear could pull him in. When he got back to his feet, the Fog had set in, and the trio slowed to a walking pace, spooked.

"I don't know about this; I can't see anything," said Derrick, stopping. "Boys, what's that?" He pointed to a rope.

One of the boys shimmied up the mountain and grabbed it. "Shit. It's a bloody rope ladder. There must be a drop in front of us."

They took off their goggles and in between clouds and fog, saw the ladder go right over a cliff face to a ledge thirty metres below. They stood silent for a minute.

"Let's find another way down," said Derrick, and they walked back up the way they had come. They took a groomed run back down the mountain to their hostel and Derrick had nervous energy when he opened the door.

"Faark, we nearly died!" Derrick giggled.

"Yiewwww! Bloody oath," yelled one of the Melburnians and he threw a can of beer at Derrick from a snow-covered balcony.

"Aussies plummet to death … What a headline," Derrick mused.

The boys regaled their story to their roommates and the tale became larger with each yarn.

Derrick had only been in Canada for a month, but the near-death experience gave him new perspective.

If I'm going to die over here, I've got to see some more of the place first.

Saying goodbye to the Victorians, Derrick caught the next bus to Fernie, a small town in the Rocky Mountains interior.

A trailer park surrounded Fernie, and as Derrick was walking through the town's centre to his hostel 'Trailer Trash' burst through a bar door and slammed straight into him.

"Fucken tourist," said the man, wrapping an arm around Derrick and pulling him to the icy tarmac below. "Out-of-towners fucken ruining the place, get the fuck out of here."

Fortunately, Derrick had made a friend on the bus, and Willem stepped in to pull him off the ground.

"Turn around and go home," said Willem to the man, with a threatening stare.

"Need your goddamn friends huh …
Motherfuckers." The man then staggered back to the trailer park yelling out profanity.

Derrick's hands stung from the slap on the ground, his clothes were sodden and he missed Australia. All he wanted just then was to go surfing with Dingo, in warm water. He was also running out of money from chasing snow bunnies and buying lift tickets. After settling into his hostel, Derrick called Geoff.

"Hey Derrick, is that you?" asked Geoff.

"Dad, it's minus 20 degrees, I'm in bum-fuck nowhere and need to get to Vancouver."

"Sounds great mate, I'll get your Mum. Hold on."

"Dad … I need your credit card number."

"You what?"

"I've run out of money, and I need to get home."

Reluctantly, Geoff handed over his credit card details and Derrick scribbled them on the back of his drawing pad.

"Tell Mum I'll speak to her later," said Derrick and he hung up the hostel's pay phone.

To his relief, Kate immediately put a couple of grand in his bank account, which he thought could last him a few more weeks, and he used Geoff's credit card to book his travel back to Vancouver.

Derrick had been in Canada for two months by the time he managed Kate's money down to the last dollar and had to leave the Rocky Mountains interior. In the early hours of the morning, a hippy driver in a van, with long hair and a backwards baseball cap, picked Derrick up to begin his long journey home to Australia.

They hadn't been on the road for five minutes before the hippy pulled into a service station for fuel.

Damn, already.

Standing at the pump, the hippy looked at Derrick and motioned him to wind down his window. "Hey bud, I don't want to leave you in the snow, but my boss isn't going to accept your dad's credit card number, he wants the actual card."

"Dude, the numbers are all you need," said Derrick, panicking. "You can take the last of my weed if you use the number and just get me to the airport."

Pulling out his last stash of weed, Derrick gave it to the driver, who quickly put it in his pocket.

"Jeez, give me a second, man. I'll call my boss."

While Derrick waited anxiously, the hippy got on his phone, paid for the gas, and then jumped back in the van.

"My man, the boss is impressed by your tenacity to leave our beautiful country. He's also looking forward to smoking your shit — I'll have you at the airport in a few hours."

Hoping to get back to some sense of normalcy, Derrick texted Dingo in Australia:

Mate, it's Derrick. I'll be home tomorrow; can you pick me up? Can't wait for waves and beer!

The hippy finally pulled his van up at Vancouver airport, with Derrick exhausted from anxiety.

"Seriously dude, if you're ever in Australia, look me up," said Derrick before hugging the hippy and walking into the terminal.

The next day, back in Sydney, Dingo sat in his station wagon sat outside arrivals and smoked a cigarette while waiting for Derrick to land.

"Sir, can move your car? You have been here too long," said a security guard.

"Two minutes, mate, I promise," said Dingo blowing smoke from his window.

Derrick walked out into the Australian sun and covered his eyes before Dingo blew his horn and stepped out of his blue Commodore wagon.

"Deezza!" shouted Dingo.

"Fuck, so good to see you," said Derrick.

"How long are you home for? Your room's still free; I just told Moose and Sharon they had to leave because you were coming back — they're pissed!" Dingo laughed.

"I reckon I'll be here until winter at least. I spent my last ten bucks leaving that joint. I've got to get a job and save for a while," said Derrick.

"Sweet," said Dingo, who then lit another cigarette and stuck his middle finger up at the security guard as they got in the car and left the airport.

Norfolk Pines lined the beach and the smell of sea spray let Derrick know he was home. They pulled into the Rat Pack, grabbed a couple of boards and ran down to their favourite peak, where the warm blue water greeted him like an old friend.

The summer sun quickly burnt Derrick's pale skin, which slowly turned a darker brown the more waves he caught and the more bricks he stacked while labouring on coastal building sites. Four months went by, and as the summer parties dwindled and the autumn air began to cool, once again Derrick turned his mind to untracked snow, but this time in New Zealand.

"Dingo, I'm gonna turn twenty in New Zealand if you want to come?" said Derrick toking on a joint on the balcony.

"New Zealand?" Dingo said staring vacantly towards the ocean.

"The mountains are as good as Canada, and it's only three hours to Queenstown."

"Come surfing with me in Europe," replied Dingo. "I'm keen to get there for the winter swell. Hossegor in France or that filthy left in Spain … Munkdaka."

"Mate, I'll do anything to stay clear of the folks. Geoff's riding me hard, telling me to study and get a career — I've paid him back, for fucks' sake."

"Get a flight to London and we'll go from there," said Dingo.

Derrick promised to meet Dingo during the European winter and a month later, he landed in Wanaka, New Zealand ready to snowboard the Southern Alps and smoke the local weed.

CHAPTER 3

It was June when Derrick arrived, and Wanaka had a cool hippy vibe where the hitchhikers were more common than cars. He got a job at an alpine resort and found a place to stay with four other backpackers. Eli was dodging Israeli conscription, Peggy was running away from Ireland, and Hamish lived in a van in the garage. Charlotte was a myth — always out when Derrick was in and vice versa.

Derrick immediately found a friend in Eli; they rarely understood each other and initially spent most days hanging out smoking the local puff. Peggy held the lease to the house and thought she ran the place. She was insanely jealous of Derrick's new friendship, but she was curt with everyone, so he didn't take it to heart. She had short red hair, drove the only green Beetle in town, could be heard from everywhere and was known to everyone.

Scoring a job at the local mountain, Derrick and his workmates met at the pub each afternoon to yarn long into the evening. Eli was ever-present, happy to be out of the house and to have a group of mates. They didn't spend much time at home, which frustrated Peggy no end. Derrick had single-handedly ruined her New Zealand dream of having house mates that wanted to spend time with her.

"She needs a man for sex," said Eli, using his best English on the way home from the pub. Derrick laughed as they tried to understand the mind of a thirty-something woman who had fled her home in Ireland.

The share house sat in a valley, beyond undulating hills that stretched from the pub along the river. The orange glow of the pub's lights began to dim as they walked further and further into the hills. When they approached the house, they quietened their laugh to a soft whisper.

"I think I can see her on the porch," said Derrick.

"I think so too," said Eli.

Twigs broke underfoot when they drew nearer, and the glow of a lit cigarette illuminated a swaying silhouette.

"Where the fuck is Derrick?" yelled Peggy with a bottle of whiskey in her hand. "Tell him he can get his things and fuck off."

Eli looked at Derrick "She said …"

"I heard, mate," said Derrick, wondering where he was going to go this late at night.

Peggy walked back in the house and slammed the door, before bursting back out and shouting some more.

"You think you can use my place as a hotel, Derrick?" she said slurring. "You take Eli everywhere you go. Taking him away from me and this house."

"Holy shit, mate! She loves you." Derrick snickered under his breath.

Eli's pupils dilated and he looked at Derrick for support. Derrick convulsed as he tried to stop laughing and he bit down hard on his tongue. They stood outside and smoked cigarettes until silence filled the house and they presumed Peggy had passed out.

"I'm getting my shit and leaving," whispered Derrick.

"Me too. I am not the man she needs to have sex with," said Eli.

Grabbing their bags, they slipped into the night as if they had never been there. They crept into a youth hostel in the centre of town, slept on the couches and then left before the staff woke in the morning.

By mid-morning, they had new accommodation with a mate on the lake. Rob was a lift operator at the local ski resort and when they weren't working, they filled his parents' home with smoke and played FIFA on PlayStation. Groove Amada's 'Vertigo' was the soundtrack to their existence, and they all became close friends.

Rob's parents were a lovely couple that lived three hours south in Dunedin, and they stayed every other weekend to keep an eye on things. Derrick only had one run-in with them, when they politely asked him to turn off the electric blanket that had been on since his arrival.

Derrick just wanted to snowboard or party, and he worked hard trying to work less. He spent most of his working day trying to convince his boss to give him more freedom.

"I'm on the cusp of turning pro," Derrick explained. "I just need more time on the mountain and if you let me work three days instead of five, you'd really be helping me out."

"Jesus, Derrick, you kill me," said the boss. "You can work in the pizza restaurant on the other side of the mountain."

Out of sight and out of mind — genius.

Grasping the new opportunity with both hands, Derrick concentrated on launching himself into the beautiful New Zealand backcountry. He couldn't be happier with the new arrangement and soon enough, he became complacent. As he'd done before in Canada, he caught an edge, but this time launching off a massive tabletop kicker. He flailed in the air upside down and knew he was in trouble. He just managed to pull round his head before slamming chest-first into the knuckle of the ramp. He heard a loud crack in his back and slid down the ramp to a stop.

Fortunately, ski patrol saw the event unfold and a medic on a snowmobile drove over and took Derrick to the doctor.

"I can't breathe," said Derrick taking short breaths. "My back." The doctor felt Derrick's back and pushed into his rib cage.

"Ahh," screamed Derrick.

"Bro, I think you've a broken rib," said the Doctor. "No joke, bro, this is no laughing matter."

Derrick winced as the Doctor made him laugh.

"You've got to be kidding," said Derrick's boss when he found out. "I'm going to fucking kill him when I see him."

Derrick returned to Australia and went straight into Kate's care. Moose and Sharon had moved into the Rat Pack and there was no chance Dingo could ask them to leave again.

Kate was over the moon to have Derrick back home, and she fussed over him relentlessly. Geoff used the time to corner him and tell him exactly what he thought of his escapades.

"When are you going to grow up, Derrick? Your mother constantly worries about you and now look at you! You're broken and at home at twenty years old. When I was your age ..."

"Oh, fuck off," said Derrick, shutting the bedroom door in Geoff's face.

"You're a loser, Derrick! The sooner you realise that the better off we'll all be," Geoff bellowed down the hallway.

"If you think yelling at him is going to do you any good, you're wrong," said Kate. "It'll only push him further away."

"I just want him to stop the transient bullshit and to get on with his life. Life's a race, not a bloody piss-up every five minutes. When is he going to have time to get an education if he keeps this up? He'll be married with kids before you know it, and then what?"

With his ear pressed to his bedroom door, Derrick quietly listened to the conversation.

He knew life was slipping slowly by, but he just wasn't quite ready to join the rest of humanity.

Why join the never-ending pursuit for happiness while I have it on my doorstep?

CHAPTER 4

After a few months at home with his parents, Derrick was depressed and needed an endorphin rush. He refused to believe he was wasting his life, but knew he was trading time for experiences. Living in the shadow of his parent's careers and their story of survival in the face of danger, he was determined to find his own meaning and purpose, and he wasn't going to find it through Geoff bullying him into conformity.

Derrick had saved enough for a flight to London, where he promised he'd meet Dingo to escape his parents' clutches, and it was cold and bleak when he arrived. He met Dingo in a South End pub where the beer was warm and soothing, and they spent a couple of days touring British pubs before they flew to Brittany, France, to surf the Atlantic coast.

On arrival, they picked up a hire car and immediately checked the surf. They hadn't long stepped out of the car before a naked Frenchman and his wife wished them Bonne Journee, on their way to play beach games on the windy and desolate beach.

"My God, it's bloody freezing," said Derrick, with his teeth chattering.

"He's playing paddle-bat with his balls out." Dingo laughed.

"At least he's got a beret on," said Derrick. "Let's go."

They walked back to the car to find that thieves had taken one of Dingo's surfboards from the roof.

"Fucken pricks!" shouted Dingo.

The Gendarmes chastised them when they reported the theft, saying it was their fault for leaving the boards unattended.

"This is stupid to leave your boards, no?" said one of the police officers.

Downhearted, they drove south to Spain and swore they wouldn't return to France.

The white country homes that dressed the French landscape soon changed to earthy terracotta tones when they approached the Spanish border. They stopped in San Sebastien where they watched the broiling, ominous clouds of a thunderstorm sweep across the crystal blue bay.

"Where should we stay?" asked Derrick.

"Let's just go to the pub and worry about it later," said Dingo. "We've got sleeping bags, we can roll up anywhere."

Derrick thought they had better set up camp somewhere, and he pulled into a rustic caravan park while Dingo swigged red wine from the bottle. Rain began to pour down, but it evaporated almost as soon as it touched the hot red earth.

"Let's stay here," said Derrick.

A bare-chested potbellied man in small green shorts emerged from a caravan and greeted them with a cigarette hanging from his mouth. "Hola," said the man. "Twenty Euros por noche."

Derrick handed over twenty Euros and the man walked them to their campsite. After setting up a children's tent they'd bought from a toy store, they threw their things inside so it wouldn't blow away. They then caught a bus into town and saddled up at a quaint tapas restaurant that resembled a whiskey bar from the prohibition era in the United States.

"It's bloody quiet round here, Dezza," said Dingo, now swigging from a beer. Tapas lined the bar, but the city was dead apart from the old sleepy woman behind the counter.

"Where is everyone?" asked Derrick.

The woman raised her eyebrows and stared with a quizzical look. "Siesta," she grumbled.

The boys spent the afternoon drinking and eating tapas and by the time people began to fill the streets in the early evening, they were drunk.

"Mate, let's go home," said Derrick, slamming down the last of his beer.

Dingo was trying his best to impress the local women with his Spanish, but he hadn't quite hit the mark.

"Yeah, let's go. I want to get up early and go surfing," said Dingo, in a state. They walked out of the bar and past a stall where Roma gypsies were selling their wares.

"You want hashish?" said an attractive young woman in a head scarf.

"Dezza, we're on … How much?" Dingo asked the woman.

The woman held Dingo's hand and placed a matchbox in his palm. "Ten Euros," she said with a smile.

Dingo was smitten and his eyes glazed over while he handed over twenty. Slowly, they made their way back to the campsite and lit a joint while gazing over the moonlit ocean.

"I reckon I could live here," said Dingo. "I could find a Spanish girl and settle down."

As lightning flickered in the distance, Derrick and Dingo slept in their board-bags with hash-fuelled dreams of dancing gypsy girls playing like movies in their minds. The next morning, they woke up without mention of a hangover and went surfing in Champagne-like conditions.

Derrick and Dingo spent weeks at a time travelling up and down the Spanish and Portuguese coast in search of waves and girls. But the backpacking surfer lifestyle came at a cost and neither of them was any good with money.

Thankfully, a flight from Spain to London was

around ten quid, so when they did run out of money, they ended up back in a London hostel searching for work.

After two years of freezing on London building sites and chasing girls on the continent, Derrick decided no more, and that he had to get back to Australia.

"Dingo!" Derrick shouted while moving bricks about a British construction site.

"What?" Dingo yelled back.

"Let's go back home — to Australia," said Derrick.

"Yes, let's definitely do that," Dingo replied.

"Before we go …" shouted Derrick from the other side of the site. "I reckon we should go to Amsterdam."

Dingo's smile then lit up the site like summer, and they both howled into the frosty air. "Mate let's get a ticket the fuck out of here," said Dingo, and he dropped the broom like a microphone before leaving stage left.

It was raining when they arrived in Amsterdam. They dropped their bags at a backpacker hostel and then found a coffee shop to warm up. An elderly woman followed them into the cafe and she sat at the table next to theirs.

Blues music gave the place a soulful feel, it was like time had slowed down and the décor had its own beat. The women reached into her coat pocket and pulled out a trumpet-sized joint, the likes of which neither Derrick nor Dingo had ever seen before.

"What is going on here?" asked Dingo with a wry smile. Nervously, they approached the marijuana bar and asked for some help.

"Can we have what she's having?" asked Derrick as he pointed to the old woman drawing back deeply on her joint.

The barman pulled out a drawer and presented them with several different blends of marijuana. They stared at the array with confused grins.

"Which one do we get?" asked Dingo. "We only have hydro or bush smoke back home."

"Try Christmas lights #5," said the barman in a thick Dutch accent. "It's an upper and you'll feel good, trust me."

Derrick bought a small bag and rolled a joint that resembled a baseball bat. He took two drags and passed it to Dingo, who was ready to burst with excitement.

"Dingo, I can't feel my feet," said Derrick after five minutes of silence. Dingo screamed in laughter, and then they both couldn't stop. The coffee shop regulars looked over as they tried to keep it together, but their bloodshot eyes and trembling bottom lips gave way to uncontrollable fits of laughter.

"You see," shouted the barman, trying to make them feel more comfortable.

The elderly woman passed a kind smile, and then drifted back to her own world with the sound of the blues amplifying the occasion.

Derrick decided he needed to go for a walk to regain his composure and after thanking the barman on their way out, they headed out into the unknown.

Immediately, he and Dingo were lost in the beauty of the streets, where harlots cooed through glass windows and bikes adorned the pavement. A cyclist rode by in leather chaps and the boys wondered what planet they had arrived on.

"We're definitely not in Kansas anymore! This place is intense, and I'm starving," said Derrick as he scanned for a kebab.

"Yeah, let's go to the pub," said Dingo.

The boys looked with youthful wonder at the crooked houses stacked up behind each other that beckoned them to keep walking. The streetscape became a mosaic of colour and sound as they walked endlessly in search of snacks.

"No wonder Picasso's paintings turned out so good," said Dingo. "This place is off its head."

In that moment, Derrick thought he had found his spiritual home and his tribe. But when he began to crash down to earth, the reality of his life became like a lead weight.

CHAPTER 5

Derrick returned to Australia and swapped the building site hard hat for a suit to begin selling mortgages for a bank. He learnt persuasion techniques akin to thievery, but the sales commission meant he could cope with the guilt. He also began art school at the Old Flour Mill and moved out of the family home into a bohemian part of the city. Kate thanked God he was finally sorting his life out but wondered what exactly an arts degree was going to do for him.

"You are going to finish this course aren't you, Derrick?" said Kate handing him the last of his possessions. "Your father's paying a lot of money to get you through this, and I don't want to see you back at home depressed."

"If I'm going spend three years studying, it might as well be something I'm interested in, hadn't it?" replied Derrick with cold determination.

I'm not going home for shit ... I'm twenty-four for God's sake.

Built in the 1700s, The Old Flour Mill was a sandstone warehouse that had thick wooden beams holding up its four floors. A spiral staircase ran throughout and led to a loft with a view of the city where the owner drank red wine in between classes. The owner stunk of stale alcohol, but his lectures captivated the audience, not least because of his drunken enthusiasm.

"Grab me a bottle of McLaren Vale?" he'd say to the students as they left his class for lunch.

Derrick learnt how to influence with colour and symbology and, while working part time at the bank, gained a thorough understanding of consumer behaviour. He spent three years honing his craft before finishing with a degree in visual communication.

The Old Flour Mill shone spectacularly on graduation day, and designers and potential employers mingled with students surrounded by their work.

"What are you going to do now?" asked a well-dressed man in his fifties while looking at Derrick's portfolio.

"I'm going to go home," replied Derrick.

"No, I mean work-wise," huffed the man, who then introduced himself as Rupert.

"I'm going to start a little magazine ... See how it goes," said Derrick, not fully understanding why he was having the conversation.

"Make it a newspaper!" Rupert replied with an excited grin and pupils the size of saucepans.

It turned out that Fake Rupert was an ex-newspaper executive whose career ended with the demise of the local rag and the beginning of social media.

"People don't want centralised news and social media; they want stories from neighbourhood journalists," he went on.

Rupert could sure mount a convincing argument and not before long, Derrick had reintroduced a retro grunge newspaper like an endangered species into the wild. But such an endeavour had a significant financial burden, and selling ad space to breathe new life into deadwood took all the negotiating skills Derrick had to offer.

Geoff had just retired, and he worked with Derrick to find new clients while Rupert would call every other day to offer his media industry guidance.

"Rupert's offered to pay for the initial print run," Derrick told Geoff after he put down the phone to him.

"Pay for it ... What if you can't pay him back? This guy will take your business," barked Geoff. "Something's not right here, mate. Let me speak to him."

Geoff took Derrick's phone and immediately called Rupert back. Derrick sat close enough that he could hear both sides of the conversation.

"Derrick," said Rupert, his seductive tone audible even from Derrick's chair.

"Rupert, it's Geoff. Now what's an old bloke like you want with a start-up paper, hey? Derrick's just finished college and you want to fuck him with debt."

"We're bringing back local media, Geoff, and we'll make millions from the ads," Rupert replied.

"Oh yeah, how much ad space have you sold then?"

A silent pause lasted just long enough so Geoff could interject before Rupert. "Thought so," Geoff said and ended the call. "He's having a lend of you, Derrick. Work with him at your peril, mate."

Rupert drifted into the ether having got the message from Geoff. But the true cost of producing legacy media and working with his dad took its toll on Derrick's mental health. After six months in print, he could afford it no more and he transformed the paper into a digital news service, where he posted social media updates for his clients.

Derrick quickly became addicted to the 24/7 news cycle, and he craved updates from the wars in the Middle East. He watched in distress as Australian deaths made the headlines and became increasingly frustrated with his inconsequential life and inability to help.

A global narrative of Islamic fundamentalists attacking the West flowed through the media, and Derrick was determined to understand why. It didn't take him long to learn of the state and non-state actors destabilising Iraq and Afghanistan and of the geopolitical factors that led to the Iranian Revolution his parents had been through. He signed up for a degree in Intelligence and Counter Terrorism and fronted up at Defence recruiting determined to make a difference.

"Full time or part time?" asked an angry-looking Army Sergeant Major at his initial interview.

"Part time," said Derrick. "I'm studying, and I'll join full time when I'm finished."

"A choco, what job are you signing up for?"

"A Combat Signaller," said Derrick. "The website said you were hiring them."

"What does that mean, then?" prodded the Sergeant Major.

Derrick began, "Well, the electromagnetic spectrum …"

"I know what the electromagnetic spectrum is," said the Sergeant Major abruptly, cutting Derrick off. "Do you know you will be up all night moving a Brigade headquarters in the bush?"

Derrick thought for a second. "No, but I'm keen."

"Bullshit, it sucks," the Sergeant Major said as he rolled back in his chair and laughed. "What you want to be is an FO, a forward observer calling in artillery rounds."

"Yeah awesome, sign me up," said Derrick.

"Done!" The Sergeant Major marched Derrick down the hall and told him to wait outside the Psychologist's office.

Derrick waited for five minutes before a muffled voice said to come in. He curiously turned the handle and pushed the door open to see a young, bearded man with glasses and cotton V-neck jumper thumbing through his paperwork.

"Take a seat on the gurney," said the Psych, pointing to the hospital bed.

Derrick hopped up and immediately lay down.

"So, you're going to be an FO?" asked the Psych.

"Yes, that's what the Sergeant Major and I were just talking about," said Derrick.

"How do you feel about killing people?" the Psych asked, looking for a reaction.

"Well, if they are shooting at me, I'll shoot back," said Derrick, staring at the roof.

"Ahh, you're a killer," said the Psych in return.

"No," said Derrick in protest and he sat bolt upright.

The Psych asked a few more random questions to determine if Derrick was a serial killer, and then marched him onto the street. "Someone will be in touch in the next couple of weeks," he said before walking back into the office.

Derrick left somewhat confused but raced home to study the role of an FO.

A week later the Sergeant Major got back in touch. "Derrick, congratulations mate, your enlistment ceremony is next Friday at midday."

"Great, so I'm going to be an FO," said Derrick.

"No, a Signaller," said the Sergeant Major before the phone line dropped dead and began to beep.

Derrick enlisted into the Army Reserves and the Commanding Officer of his new unit welcomed him on board.

"Mate, it's the stand-down period for Christmas and New Year, no one's at work. Don't bother turning up until you get your dates for basic training. We'll see you when you've completed your course," said the CO.

Jeez, not much of an anti-climax.

Derrick waited to begin military training and continued to study and post updates to social media, but a call from a client caught him off guard.

"Hello mate," said the client in a British accent. "I need someone to write ads, to win business from our marketing efforts. Is that you Derrick, are you good at that?" said the client playing to Derrick's ego.

"I like to think so," said Derrick with laugh.

"How much money do you make doing that for yourself?" asked the client. "Come and work with me and we'll make millions, I promise."

All Derrick had to do was write online ads to lure tech-savvy IT developers to click and engage, the consultants did the rest. Derrick thought it was a 'win-win' and with a cheeky laugh from the client, he joined the team.

Over the next few weeks, money started pouring in, but it was a soulless existence. The sales board tallied in hundreds of thousands, but Derrick didn't care. He wanted to change the world and joining the military was the itch he had to scratch.

Finally, his date for basic training arrived and he eagerly said goodbye to the monotony of office life and handed in his resignation.

On a cold and drizzly winter's morning, he boarded a military bus with several other nervous civilians bound for 'Kapooka', the home of the soldier.

CHAPTER 6

All soldiers must go through 'Kapooka'; where recruits change bed sheets too slowly and the incorrect door knock procedure draws the ire of the instructors.

"Stop!" screeched a Corporal as Derrick marched to the shower on his first night. "Do you like blinding me, recruit?"

Confused, Derrick stood with his heart racing.

"Why is the white drawstring outside your shorts? Go back to your room, tuck it in, and start over," the Corporal yelled.

"Stop!" he yelled again just as Derrick marched away. "Clench your fists when you're marching, or you'll soon find the Sergeant Major's pace stick in there."

Directing staff gave frequent verbal encouragement, and "hurry up and un-fuck yourself," quickly became the favourite phrase of Derrick's platoon.

Recruits had seven minutes to shower, brush their teeth and get ready for bed. They yelled the national anthem along a hallway and then the directing staff turned out the lights. The morning routine was just as panicked, and recruits rushed to the hallway with bed sheets across their shoulders, to prove they hadn't slept on a made bed. Instructors told them what dress to get into, to remake their beds and to form up on the parade ground before they marched them to the day's lessons. The recruits learnt to march, use different weapon systems, and survive on ration packs that had expiration dates like Derrick's birthday.

Derrick's sense of purpose was written across his face, similar to his grin when he recounted the day's hilarity before sleep. When his mate King Shitter, who was named after his love of cleaning toilets, took a knee in between him and a left-handed rifleman on a patrol one night, he couldn't have known he would laugh about it until the day he died. The 'enemy' crept up and ambushed their position while the three spoke quietly behind a berm. They opened fire in return, and King Shitter found himself in between two rifles ejecting hot spent cartridges straight down his shirt.

"Cease fire… fucken cease fire," King Shitter yelled as he hopped about wildly trying to release the shells from his shirt and pants.

After six weeks of hard training, Derrick marched out of Kapooka and into the Signals Regiment, where life wasn't quite as amusing. But he was determined to use the posting as a pathway to finishing his degree, transferring to the Intelligence Corps, then trying his luck at becoming an Officer.

Derrick was optimistic and was talking through his plan with King Shitter at a bar, when an attractive woman on crutches caught his eye.

"What happened to you?" asked Derrick as she hopped by.

"I broke my kneecap playing tennis," said the woman with a Californian twang.

"Sounds like you need a drink," said Derrick.

The woman laughed and rolled her eyes. "Oh my God, that's bad! But do you mind if I sit here?" she asked, resting her crutches on Derrick's table before sitting next to him.

"What do you guys do, and why are you at the pub at 2 pm on a Wednesday?" she quizzed.

"Well, we could ask the same of you, but we're in the Army," Derrick bleated. "We just finished a course, and we have a few days off. Hi … I'm Derrick and this is King Shitter."

"Hey, I'm Charlie, and why's he called King Shitter?"

It turned out Charlie was quite well to do; her parents were lawyers at a top firm in Sydney and they paid for her education at an Ivy League college in the U.S. She was a semi-professional tennis player who spent more time on the beach than on the court. Immediately in love, Derrick chased Charlie day and night, but she played hard to get and would often refuse his calls. The Army also sent him away with increasing regularity, and he focused on work to stave off his romantic pursuit.

Derrick travelled to Melbourne in winter, to train in hi-wire personnel recovery. He scaled telegraph poles like electrified stalagmites, and came down to zap his mates with wind up K-Phones while they built telecommunication networks for gun pits. A favourite trick was to wind up the K-Phone and dip the electrodes in the stream of a mate's piss. A seventy-five-volt whack to the knob then warmed the coldest of hearts. It was harmless digger fun.

After the long days out in the cold, Derrick and his course mates went to the hipster pub scene on Brunswick Street to debrief on the day's activities.

"Strippers?" said Derrick after his fifth pint. A collective cheer went up and they made their way through the miserable weather to a popular but seedy night spot.

"Hello," said a Russian dancer to Derrick's friend.

"Can you do me a favour?" said his friend to the dancer. The dancer raised a brow and leant in closer to listen. "Derrick's a bit kinky, and he likes to be slapped." The dancer looked at Derrick and smiled.

"Hey beautiful?" said Derrick as the dancer came closer.

She stepped forward and with an open palm slapped him fair across the chin. His eyes rolled back, and it was all he could do to stay conscious. A bouncer came over and immediately shoved him out the door. His mates roared with laughter, and they left the club to buy him a well-deserved beer at the Fox and Hound.

Melbourne was fast becoming Derrick's favourite Australian city, but so was everywhere the Army sent him. He travelled the country over a couple of years and Charlie seemed happy to have a fly-in, fly-out kind of boyfriend. He ended his lease in Sydney and stayed on barracks or with Charlie … when she let him.

"Of course, you can stay here when you're back home," said Charlie. "You can take me out and watch me play tennis."

But the agreement would only last a few days before Charlie sent him away — almost as regularly as the Army did.

"Derrick, can you fuck off? I need a good night's sleep."

His continued stay on base also irritated the civilian contractors who ran base administration, and they began to make his life difficult.

"I'm sorry Derrick, the rooms are fully booked, and we don't have a vacancy for months."

Derrick knew it was bullshit, but he had little room for negotiation and moved into a shared apartment with a pianist named Penelope. He swore it would be the last time he rented in Sydney, but the location was good, and he could run along the coast each afternoon.

One afternoon, Derrick was listening to his headphones after his jog, when he opened the bathroom door to hop in the shower.

"Derrick, no…" screamed Penelope, already in the shower. But Derrick's momentum carried him past the point of no return and Penelope's skeletal figure grasped for a towel, like in a scene from Hitchcock's Psycho.

Reversing quickly out, Derrick closed the door. "Shit," he said softly, before grabbing a beer from the fridge to erase the memory. *I'll watch the surf for a bit and give Penelope time to recover.*

Derrick walked out to the point and watched the rolling swell smash onto the rocks below. He was lost in thought when a melody swirled on the sea breeze, and it lured him home where Penelope was tinkering away on the keys.

"Sorry about that," said Derrick when he walked back into the apartment. Penelope smiled shyly and continued playing her intoxicating music.

A storm had rolled in from the coast when Derrick got to work the next morning. Black Hawk loadmasters were getting qualified, and Derrick's boss told his section to lend a hand.

"Go to all-round defence when we land, then throw smoke from the bush to mark your location," instructed the Loadie. "We'll circle around and pick you up when we see smoke."

The Loadie marshalled Derrick and his section onto the air frame, and they took off from base. They landed somewhere in the middle of the bush, where the Loadie gave the thumbs-up to unbuckle their straps and get ready to exit.

The first to leave was Derrick's mate, Emu. As he leapt out, he looked back. "Fuck," mouthed Emu before facing his fate and jumping out to land on his stomach. The storm that rolled in off the coast had turned the bush dust into a thick and soupy swamp, and Emu dove straight in.

Derrick got lucky and jumped on hard sandstone, where he faced out against an enemy of smiling trees. The helicopter took off and the screaming engines drowned out Derrick's laughter as the mud splattered everywhere.

"The pilot's a dickhead," said Emu after silence had returned, and they ran into the bush to 'pop smoke'. They repeated the serials over and over to ensure the Loadie got qualified. Derrick became good mates with Emu that day, and they agreed being a reservist was the best — like being in a comedy club but being paid to do cool shit — and only if you wanted to.

When they returned from the Black Hawk flight, the CO asked, "Emu, do you want to do an exercise in Adelaide?"

"When is it Sir?" Emu replied.

"It's over June and July," the CO replied.

Emu reclined in his chair filthy with mud, put his hands behind his head and smiled. "Adelaide in winter, Sir. I'll check with the wife to see if she'll let me go. Sounds like an awesome opportunity though!"

Derrick's unit taught him military history and to be part of the serving family. He learned of the Battle of Beersheba and researched the importance of key terrain, logistics nodes and fuel supply, like the water wells needed to sustain their horses. He also learnt about misinformation and the campaign that deceived Turkish planners.

"With rifles slung and bayonets in their hands, ANZAC soldiers on horseback rode under enemy fire to storm the trenches and capture Beersheba."

Now in his early thirties, ANZAC day had new clarity for Derrick and that year he attended a ceremony that lit up a dark dawn on the beach.

"Did you see the PM getting smashed with the rugby boys the other night?" Derrick asked the local politician representing his electorate. "Disgraceful behaviour, having fun with the lads," he continued joking.

The Deputy Prime Minister smiled and sipped his tea while the rest of the crowd shared a gunfire breakfast and morning froth to commemorate the fallen.

The dawn ceremony was moving, and as the sun set on a solemn day Derrick penned his final essay, which marked the end of study and Army reserves, and the beginning of full-time service.

CHAPTER 7

Derrick flew into Queensland a couple of weeks after Anzac Day, and a nondescript van picked up him and two others at Brisbane airport. Derrick had transferred to intelligence, and they drove to a base tucked into the mountains like a scene from an Ian Fleming novel. He found his bearings running through rainforest, where he startled Pretty-Faced Wallabies and made turtles take cover in glistening creeks.

On his first day at work, the students were welcomed to country by an Aboriginal Elder who washed them in smoke before the day's briefings began. Derrick collapsed in his room twelve hours later, where he checked to see if Charlie had messaged.

I'm pregnant, read the first message from Charlie.
What? replied Derrick.

Charlie sent a photo of the pregnancy test but Derrick was confused.

What am I looking for I can't see a pink line? he sent back.

Well, I can. Now I'll have to pay for an abortion and I'm sending you the bill, she messaged.

Derrick's anxiety peaked, but he also thought it could be a ruse, so he picked up the phone to talk through the situation with Charlie.

"Are you sure?" asked Derrick. "I can't see anything."

"I can see the line," Charlie replied.

"What do you want to do?"

"I'll have to get an abortion, won't I?"

"You don't want to keep it?"

"No, Derrick, I don't."

"Ok, I'll support you, whatever your decision." Derrick didn't know what to say and Charlie hung up without letting him finish.

Are you ok? Derrick texted the next day.

I am fine now Derrick, you fucking asshole, replied Charlie a day later. *I took loads of contraception pills and I've had my period.*

This relationship is so fucking hot and cold, Derrick whispered to himself.

Every other month Derrick flew to Sydney to see Charlie, but the tyranny of distance only made the minor romantic dramas worse.

"What are you doing up there, Derrick? Why can't you come home on the weekends?"

"Charlie, I can't keep arguing about this, I spend all my free time marking up maps and studying, there's a shitload of work I have to do."

"This Army shit sucks. I'm going to a festival on the weekend and it would have been nice if you could have come."

"I'll make it up to you. I'll take you away at the end of the year."

Derrick wasn't going to let his relationship get in the way of his new career but he still wanted Charlie to be proud of what he was doing.

Why doesn't she understand I have to do this?

Before long, it was the end of the year and Derrick had six weeks leave but it came with a stern warning from the RSM, "Do not get arrested."

Derrick drove down to Sydney, looking forward to a summer of debauchery, and he'd booked a trip to California with Charlie where he planned to surf and party like there was no tomorrow. But first he spent Christmas with Geoff and Kate.

"So, who's this new Girl Charlie you're going to California with?" asked Geoff at the dinner table with a glass of red.

"At least it's a girl and not Dingo," Kate interjected.

"I haven't seen Dingo in years," said Derrick. "Charlie studied in the US, she a tennis player."

"A tennis player, any good?" Geoff inquired.

"She's semi-professional."

"Semi," howled Geoff before bursting in laughter.

"Kate plays tennis socially. You should have a hit, love."

"Don't listen to him. We want you to have a nice time in the US and we're ever so proud of what you've achieved."

"Whatever you do, don't let this girl de-rail you. If she loves you, she'll come along for the ride."

They arrived in the U.S. early in the morning and went straight to the beach before checking into their hotel at Newport Beach.

"I'm not going out tonight," said Charlie, still tired from the flight.

"What?" said Derrick. "We just got here … I'm going surfing and then to the bar."

Derrick left and went to Huntington Beach to watch surfers snake through the pier and introduced himself into the local bar scene while Charlie watched the Kardashians on TV.

After a couple of days of the same routine, Derrick came through the hotel door in sunglasses and a tie-dyed t-shirt. "Hey, I got some food," he said in an American accent.

"I don't want any food; I ate hours ago!" Charlie shouted from bed.

"Jesus, I'm just trying to be nice," he replied with a drunken grin.

"Go to sleep, I'll talk to you in the morning." Charlie rolled over and turned off the light, while Derrick got into bed and wondered what he had got himself into.

They stayed for two weeks, but the holiday was nothing like Derrick had planned. Charlie wasn't impressed either, with him or with being back in the U.S., and by the time they got home to Sydney they'd stopped talking to each other.

Derrick had one week of leave left and much to his surprise, Charlie decided they'd go out with her friends. "So, you're happy to go out now?" he asked, filled with resentment.

"You knew I lived in the U.S. to play tennis and you didn't take me once," Charlie said, glaring at him. "We're going out with my friends and doing what I want to do now."

Fuck, you didn't ask or want to... thought Derrick, recounting the trip. He knew he was being shaped into what Charlie wanted him to be, but he was blinded by lust and still young enough not to see through the trees.

"How good are Tim's shoes?" said Charlie, pointing to the ground once they met her mates at a bar.

"I don't give a fuck about Tim's shoes," said Derrick, filthy with the situation.

"Okay, let's go." Charlie marched him out of the bar and verbally sprayed him on the footpath. "If you don't start acting like a normal person, this relationship is over. Give me a cigarette," she demanded.

"I don't think so," said Derrick in disbelief.

"Well, I'll see you at home. I'm staying with my friends!" She turned and left Derrick on the footpath.

I'm done with this shit, he thought, and he got his things from her place, got in his car, and drove off in the dark. *Fuck Sydney, I am not coming back here*.

He drove two hours north before the police directed him to stop at a roadside breath testing station.

"Got your licence, mate?" asked the cop. "Why did you try and go round me?"

"I didn't," said Derrick steaming with stale alcohol.

"Mate, you stink of piss," said the cop as he looked into Derrick's eyes. "Blow into this and count to ten."

Derrick blew into a straw and the police officer told him to wait.

"Sir, right now you are under arrest and coming with me." The police officer drove Derrick to the local police station where they promptly charged him, then asked him to leave.

"Where am I?" asked Derrick.

"You can get a cab into town, but don't think about getting your car," said the officer.

"We drove 45 minutes from my car! What town is this?" asked Derrick, panicking.

"Ask the cab driver. You are now free to leave until your court date."

Derrick caught a cab to his car, parked in the emergency lane on the highway, whereupon he jumped in the tray and went straight to sleep.

A week later, Derrick arrived back at work and began his first day feeling the least bit intelligent. He confessed all to the RSM. "Sir, I fucked up."

"How bad is it?" said the RSM.

"I've been done for DUI."

"At least you know shit only gets worse when it rolls downhill."

Unaware of what his fate may be, the next few weeks were solemn at best. Derrick prayed to God the Almighty that the Army wouldn't kick him out, and he pressed on with his training.

The military paperwork to punish him took weeks to finalise before the RSM marched Derrick to the CO of his training unit.

"Derrick, I'm disappointed you're in front of me but thank God you didn't kill anyone," said the CO. "You're a good soldier and it'd be a great shame if this ruined your career. If I were you, I'd put this behind you and invest in your training."

The CO took away any opportunity for him to be deployed or promoted in the next year, but Derrick kept his job. He'd learnt his lesson and became more driven over the next few months, working harder than ever through the long nights and intense scrutiny.

He emerged with a posting order, which was to remain where the white sand beaches merged into the horizon. Queensland.

"Better than Sydney," said Derrick to his mates after completing his training.

"Waves and babes," said his pasty and square jawed mate the Russian. "Derrick, make sure when hot babes are at your house I am there too. We should have pool party and invite girls from Gold Coast."

Although he'd lived in Australia since he was ten, the Russian still had a thick accent, and his tone was as abrupt as if he'd just stepped off a flight from Moscow.

"They're too busy looking in the mirror," said Derrick quickly dispelling the Russian's hopes.

"Call them ... they will come. This is Queensland, beautiful girls one day, perfect the next."

Derrick had led his mates to believe his life revolved around hedonism and debauchery, but the DUI charge had subdued his former lifestyle. He was alone, lived on base and needed time to right the wrongs of his bad decisions. He buried himself in work.

It was banking and marketing that had taught Derrick persuasion and influence, but he weaponised his skills through the dark art of psychological operations. He became obsessed with behavioural change and how graphics could support warfare.

When the Islamic State seized the city of Mosul in Iraq, Derrick saw first-hand how terrorists used information operations. The imagery told a brutal narrative, that death awaits those who stand in their way. Their messaging campaign was slick, horrific, and amplified the size of their force. Iraqi Soldiers just walked away from their posts and handed the city over.

In a secure basement devoid of windows or plants, Derrick worked on operations in the Middle East. He looked for trends and insights that a deployed force might be interested in and fed his analysis through to ground force elements.

"We're looking for intent," said the operations officer. "The Islamic State are targeting Iraqis with their messaging. We need to know if they like it or hate it, and what they are saying about it. Most importantly, what are they saying about the Coalition? The Militia is on our side now; we need to know if this changes."

"How can we influence what the public's receiving?" asked Derrick.

"That's not our job, we're the collectors," said the officer.

"So, you want social media analysis of the week's violence?"

"We analyse information to inform operations, for fuck's sake, Derrick."

"Information we can't influence … Sounds like a stitch-up to me," Derrick replied, rolling his eyes.

"Just make sure your product is ready by Friday," the officer barked as he left the basement.

Derrick spent six months screening videos and images from Islamic State and Shia Militias and many of the images seared to his memory; like when a young boy ran from his parents in Palestine to join the fight against the Islamic State. Armed thugs murdered the boy at the Syrian border while he tried to join a Militia. They broadcast the boy's death on the internet as part of an influence campaign. That vision burnt deeper than most.

CHAPTER 8

When Derrick got his driver's licence back, he regained his freedom and moved into a high-rise apartment overlooking the Brisbane River. Before work each morning, he ran through the Botanical Gardens, along the river and finished with a swim in the pool.

Due to deploy to the Middle East, he had a few boxes to check before his departure. Chemical, Biological, Radiological and Nuclear Defence, known as CBRN-D training was one such box. The Army had gassed Derrick before, and he was confident he knew what he was in for.

"Right you lot, stop the chatter," said the British instructor. "You're here because the Army wants you to be, so sit down."

"State and non-state actors use chemical and biological agents in peace time and in war to meet their political objectives. In 2017, assassins killed Kim Jong Nam with VX nerve agent in Malaysia. In 2018, the Syrian Army dropped chlorine bombs on their own citizens, and in the same year in the UK the nerve agent Novichok nearly killed former double agent Sergei Skripal and his daughter Yulia, and the list goes on ..."

The CBRN-D presentation projected onto the screen in front of them and an audible groan resonated through the classroom. The door closed, the lights dimmed, and an unenthused voice started the first lesson. Blistered skin and dilated pupils flashed up on the screen and a graphic recount of history accompanied the painful images. The instructor gave the students Diazepam and Atropine pens to play with while the hours slowly ticked by.

"Derrick," whispered the Russian. "Pass me the Diazepam pen, I'll inject myself to go to sleep."

"Inject me," said Derrick and they wrestled for the pen.

"Boys!" the instructor yelled.

"How do I go to the toilet in my chemical suit?" said the Russian.

"You don't! You wait or go in the suit."

"What about number two?" said the Russian and the classroom laughed.

"Half your luck if you never use these suits," said the instructor calmly. "Chemical attacks kept us in them for months. The Islamic State shelled the Kurds, and the Syrians, with chlorine and mustard gas. The smoke burns every orifice of everybody, no discrimination."

"How do I know if my suit's on properly?" said the Russian.

"You'll find out tomorrow when the gas burns your eyes." The instructor then dismissed the class, and Derrick walked out with the Russian.

"See you tomorrow, Derrick." The Russian smiled. "Bring a cup for your tears."

The next morning Derrick and the Russian turned up at the classroom to find the British instructor passing out suits and masks.

"Grab a suit, boots, mask and gloves and get them on," the instructor said. "If the mask and gloves fit, put them in your sack with an extra canister. Keep your suit and boots on, then form up into three ranks.

"Platoon … attention," the instructor screamed, and the class snapped their boots together and stood stiffly in the heat.

"Platoon … le…ft turn." The formed body turned 90 degrees and stared up a road that led into the bush. "In two kilometres, on your right-hand side, you will see the training staff who will lead you to the smokehouse."

"Platoon … quick … march." They marched towards the smokehouse and their uniforms became heavy from the sweat.

"Running … change …" After running two kilometres in 35-degree heat it was clear who'd been drinking the night before.

"You lot stink like a fucking brewery," the instructor yelled as they neared the smokehouse. The training staff led the platoon past burnt and blackened trees from bushfires to the smokehouse where it stood in a clearing.

"Right, platoon," the instructor yelled. "There isn't a breath of wind, but we will pretend it is coming from the south." The instructor pointed along the bush track they had just walked down.

"On the words of command, GAS, GAS, GAS, you'll take one last breath, point your ass to the wind, don your mask, your gloves and seal your suit. Now turn your attention to the training staff."

"GAS, GAS, GAS!" the instructor yelled at the top of his lungs. The training staff yelled the words of command, and they faultlessly completed the drill while the platoon watched on. It was then their turn to practise. The platoon split into three sections and began working in pairs. Derrick and the Russian teamed up to make sure their drills and seals were tight.

"GAS, GAS, GAS!" the instructor yelled, and the course stuck their ass to the wind and donned their suits.

"You look good," said the Russian like in a scene from the Chernobyl disaster. Derrick purged his mask, and the Russian sealed his hood. Derrick checked over the Russian and once training staff thought the platoon was competent, they began a ten-minute fitness session.

Exhausted and dripping in sweat, Derrick's section stacked up in a line against the smokehouse.

"Right, close your eyes and put a hand on the person to your front's shoulder. When you think he has entered the house, hold your breath …" the instructor yelled. The smokehouse door opened, and the instructor led them inside.

"GAS, GAS, GAS!" yelled the instructing staff simultaneously.

Derrick was last in and immediately out of breath. He could barely get the words of command out, "Gas, gas, gas," he whimpered and reflexively took a breath. The gas asphyxiated him momentarily and stung his wet skin. He frantically donned his mask and purged in a panic. Directing staff had already cleared the Russian, who was doing star jumps to prove his seals were working. Derrick tapped him to check him over.

"You look like you have lost your toys, Derrick," said the Russian through his mask.

"Fuck you mate, just make sure my suit is tight," said Derrick in the middle of flight or fight panic.

The Russian grabbed Derrick and inspected his suit.

"You're fine, but your eyes look cooked."

"You're not leaving the smokehouse until you complete a canister change and do push ups and burpees," yelled the instructor.

The section danced then changed canisters, before finally having their masks removed and being told to walk out with their eyes open. Grown men were in tears and mucus streamed from their noses. The sting eventually faded and after five minutes Derrick could see clearly once more.

"It tastes like warheads," said Derrick. "The hot ones."

"They should make more smoke," said the Russian.

Almost as soon as Derrick got rid of his gas mask, his Platoon Sergeant called him to say he was deploying on an exercise in the morning.

"We leave for the RAAF base at first light, so make sure you kit is ready to go," said the Sergeant.

By lunch the next day, Derrick was ready to go to war with a fictitious enemy in the heart of the Australian jungle.

Derrick and graphic designer Bulldog worked through hundreds of ideas testing their effectiveness, much like a regular design agency would do but with graver consequences. They worked their communications and media products through a review board, and when the CO gave them the green light, the operators used their work in the field.

"Bulldog, we need to demoralise the enemy," said Derrick once briefed on the exercise situation. "These guys are just puppets with a master." He drew a couple of thumbnails in his note pad and put them in front of Bulldog. "Can you come up with a couple of designs that reflect a puppet on strings, dancing for his master? And one like a sock puppet, but a bit more graphic," said Derrick with a wink.

Bulldog laughed as he flipped through the thumbnails and knew exactly what to do. A beast of a character at 6.5 feet tall and just as wide, when Bulldog got excited his red hair bristled and he looked like a Scottish Marauder about to devour prey.

After a few hours, with a Cheshire grin Bulldog summoned Derrick to his laptop. Derrick looked down to what was a graphic novel in the waiting. A powerful anti-hero's fist firmly implanted into the backside of a guerrilla fighter shone from the screen. The fighter depicted as a puppet of the 'State' was exactly the extreme Derrick was looking for. He added some text and put it aside. He needed two other designs that were a bit less confronting before unleashing the trump card.

At the review board Derrick briefed his concepts to the CO and operations staff. "Sir, the two designs shown will demoralise supporters of the enemy and circulate as memes through various media channels. They'll also be produced in print and be placed in high traffic areas," said Derrick.

The first image was of a voodoo doll dancing on strings with text that said, 'Puppets get pricked'. The second was of a disfigured Pinocchio with big bold text that said, 'You Lied'.

"Approved, and circulate widely," said the CO.

"Sir, the last product goes a bit further and is intended to be placed on doors at night," said Derrick. "Villagers will see the posters and share it through their networks. All of these posters are attributed to a group that villagers can get behind." He changed the slide, and an almighty roar went up from headquarters staff.

"Cleared! Give these posters to the teams heading out tonight. And get some stickers made up and put them everywhere. The resistance is coming!" said the CO with a laugh.

Derrick was in his element and once the campaign had taken hold, he proposed dropping toy gimps into the area of operations from a C-130 Hercules. That idea found its way to a two-star general, who stopped it. The General then completely lost his shit when he saw the fist-in-ass poster.

As the exercise began to quieten, news of a suicide devastated the entire command. One of their own, a soldier and veteran, a father and husband, whose service to country had ended too soon.

"Corporal Berkshire was an outstanding soldier and mate to a lot of you," said the CO. As we support his family and take care of his final wishes … talk to your mates, and talk to Corporal Berkshire's mates. Do not suffer in silence."

The CO's pain was visible and he offered immediate support to those who needed it.
"I'll make sure you're on the next available flight home to spend time with your family and friends, the exercise is over," he said.

The reality of serving in the military struck Derrick hard, and he found it difficult to understand what his colleagues were going through. As he crossed the tarmac to a waiting C-17 on his way home his troop sergeant called, which was a much-needed distraction from his spiralling thoughts.

"Derrick!" shouted the Sergeant. "How do you feel about sailing around Southeast Asia with a naval Task Group?"

"I thought I was going to the Middle East, Sergeant?" replied Derrick solemnly.

"We need someone in the Task Group, and you're it," the Sergeant replied.

Derrick suspected his unit had removed him from the Middle East trip because he'd put in for a transfer from soldier to officer and he was being punished for being a traitor. He didn't hate the idea of sailing through the region, but Derrick was angry he wouldn't get a chance to undermine the likes of those who murdered the Palestinian boy.

"Okay, Sarge," said Derrick, deflated.

"Bulldog and Russian are going," said the Sergeant as a peace offering.

"When do I leave?" said Derrick.

"The ship leaves Sydney in two weeks."

"Well, I'm going on leave until then." Derrick hung up and messaged Charlie.

I'll be in Sydney for the next couple of weeks, can I come see you?

CHAPTER 9

Two weeks later, Australia quickly became a spot on the horizon, and the Task Group sailed through the Timor Sea to Dili Harbour, where they dropped anchor. Small spot fires lit up the hills and veterans of the East Timor Crisis told stories of the kind people and unforgiving landscape.

"That ridge is where I fell and broke my back," said a soldier with a blank gaze on the quarterdeck. "Fell with my pack on and compressed my lower spine. The boys got me down on a stretcher."

Derrick drew back on his cigarette and stared into the distance. The hot breeze kissed his neck and then the sun dipped into the black inky water. The grumble of engines regained his focus and the ship steamed towards Indonesia.

The Task Group came alongside in Jakarta at dawn. The Army had set up a skills demonstration across from their berth and a military band welcomed them to Indonesia.

"I'm going into the city," said Derrick from his bunk. Bulldog and the Russian were still fast asleep, and he didn't get a reply. He showered and got ready, then walked across the ship, then down a flight of stairs to the gangway. He stood next to the duty officer and looked out the port door to see an Indonesian Sergeant threating a private with a black stick.

"Good to see standards are being maintained here too," said Derrick, more interested in talking to the attractive duty officer.

"The soldiers are being punished if they don't complete drills correctly," said the duty officer. "Our military's gone way too soft."

"Righto Maggie Thatcher, well I'm off for breakfast beers," said Derrick and he bounced down the gangway to meet up with some others who had the same idea. They made their way through the smog and crowded streets and ended up at a posh hotel in the financial district.

"Fancy the cat poo coffee?" asked Derrick as he scanned the menu.

A neatly dressed policy advisor from the task group suddenly retched, nearly spitting her drink across the table.

"No thank you!" she spluttered.

"It's good for you," Derrick explained. "The coffee cherries ferment in a cat's stomach and then they're brewed."

"I feel sick," said the woman, turning pale.

They had been at sea for a couple of weeks, but the port visit to Jakarta was only a day trip for international engagement, well above Derrick's pay grade. So, after a couple of breakfast beers, they poked around town before setting sail for Malaysia in the evening. Derrick was back on watch as they sailed, but apart from confirming a few friendly aircraft sorties out of Singapore, he was bored and looking forward to a few days off in Malaysia.

Port Klang was the gateway to Kuala Lumpur, but other than vague memories of it as a child, Derrick knew little about it. He, Bulldog, and the Russian took a cab from the port and made their way to the Petronas's Towers in the city.

"I'm not going up there," said the Russian. "Too many people."

"Yeah, I can't be bothered either," said Derrick. The Malaysian Grand Prix was in town and there were people everywhere.

"It's nearly lunch, let's go and eat," said Bulldog.

Derrick brought up Google and searched: restaurants near me? "Google thinks Bukit Bintang is work a look," he said.

The three of them walked through the shadows of clothes drying from apartment windows, with the smell of chilli crab permeating the air.

"The Irish Bar looks good," said Bulldog as they walked down a hawker's gauntlet designed to separate tourists from their cash. They walked into the pub and saw most of the Task Group had the same idea.

"Boys!" a sailor yelled. "Get in here!"

Like flies to shit, the bar packed out within minutes.

Two beautiful women with bright blue eyes and dark hair joined the party and sat across from Derrick's table. They smoked shisha and a nervous young sailor asked if he could join them.

"Of course, sit with us darling," cooed one of the girls and she passed him the pipe.

The young sailor took a deep drag of apple flavoured smoke and blew a thick cloud into the night sky. "That's amazing!" He coughed, and the girls laughed.

They then looked at Derrick, Bulldog, and the Russian. "You want to try?" they asked.

The Russian looked at the sailor and said, "Little baby," he then took the pipe from the sailor's hands. "Where are you from?" the Russian asked.

"Tehran," said one of the women.

"Iran," said the Russian loudly.

"You have been?"

"No, but I like Persian food."

"Derrick, come join us. These girls are from Iran. Derrick's parents were kicked out of Iran," said the Russian, putting his arm around one of the girls and Bulldog sat next to the other.

The defeated young sailor watched on as Derrick moved in and began to exaggerate the story of his parents' escape, much to the delight of girls.

"What's your Instagram?" said one of the girls, scrolling through her phone.

Suddenly, Derrick thought Charlie had set a honey trap. He hadn't spoken to her since leaving Australia, having loosely gotten back together. The last few messages he'd received were a stream of abuse about who he followed on the platform.

Who the hell is the MILF Hunters? read Charlie's text with a barrage of lewd pictures.

I don't know what you are talking about? replied Derrick.

You follow them, mate … Charlie sent back.

I've got an app that 'follows' people that 'follow' me, Derrick explained. It took weeks at sea for the battle to abate.

Derrick decided to leave the Russian and Bulldog before tempting fate by swapping details with the girls. The Task Group was leaving in the morning, and he was sure the boys would regale him with their tales of debauchery on the quarterdeck.

The South China Sea was still and lifeless when they sailed silently to Manila and Derrick had little to report on workwise. The Chinese were celebrating Golden Week, and the Task Group travelled uninterrupted past some newly man-made islands. They sailed south to Subic Bay after a brief visit to the Philippine capital, where the scenery was Jurassic and the Free Port Zone set up to satisfy thirsty and lusting sailors.

Derrick walked off the ship into a scrum of street vendors selling butterfly knives, tasers and sunglasses.

"Aargh …" screamed Derrick as the left side of his body contracted, on fire. "God damn it!" he shouted, looking back at the Russian.

"It works well," said the Russian holding a taser, and he handed the hawker a fistful of pesos.

"You want sex?" said the vendor, slowly thumbing through the bills. "I get you girl or boy?" The Russian stopped him before a finger went through the hole his thumb and index finger had made.

"Ask that question again and your finger will go up your …"

"Let's go, mate," said Derrick and he moved the Russian to a bar.

Subic Bay's girlie bars and sex industry thrived off the back of its Naval history and prostitution seemed part of the landscape. The US Navy base closed in the nineties, though the people who remained bought bars and took their slice of 'Sin City'. Derrick and the Russian entered a club where half-naked girls lined up to get them drinks. The girls wore numbers, and their tops read 'Cheap Drinks and Fun!'

"Is prostitution legal?" asked the Russian.

"No, and their President kills people for less," said Derrick.

The pair moved to an open-air bar to watch the waves of personnel roll off the ship and two young sailors walked in after them.

"First we're getting tattoos, then let's hit the girlie bars in Barrio Barretto," said one of the sailors, boasting loudly.

A Filipino waitress walked over to Derrick and leaned in as if to take his order.
"Don't let the girls get you drunk," she said softly in an ominous warning before walking off behind the bar.

Meanwhile, the Russian had spotted an old friend and had decided to re-engage.

"It's the baby from the Irish Bar in Malaysia," shouted the Russian. "You didn't get your girl and you now have to pay for them, uh?" He laughed and put his arm around the sailor, who winced with a nervous smile.

The quarterdeck gossips held the Russian in high regard after the visit to Malaysia. Rumour had it he left the Irish bar with an Iranian beauty and was the last person back on the ship before it departed for Manila.

Derrick had developed a sense for trouble after his issues with Charlie and the DUI charge, and he didn't have a second chance to fuck up. He motioned to the Russian to exit the bar and to leave the sailors to their own devices. Bulldog had just texted and he'd sent a picture of an idyllic beachside bar.

Catch a tuk tuk to Geronimo Street. I'm at the Tinker Taylor Hotel.

"Rip it up boys!" Derrick said to the sailors as he high-fived them on the way out. "What's the bet they're the first casualties of the port visit?" Derrick said as he and the Russian jumped into a rickshaw and sped over the mountains.

Bulldog was sitting at the bar when they arrived and a fierce-looking woman with a missing tooth was giving him a shoulder massage. He glanced over to Derrick and the Russian as they walked in.

"This is what life's all about," he shouted with a bottle of beer in hand. "Girls appear from nowhere and start stroking your neck!"

Just like clockwork two provocative silhouettes sauntered towards Derrick and the Russian.

"They are not for sex," said the woman massaging Bulldog. "You buy them a drink and they will flirt with you."

"And I'll suck your cock," whispered one of the women into Derrick's ear.

Derrick smiled and bought a round of drinks while the woman's hand began to comb through his hair.

Charlie will fucking kill me.

Soon, more people arrived and the conversations got louder and more exaggerated. The drink and the atmosphere took control of their senses, and they partied until they dropped under the white glow of a tropical moonlit beach.

Derrick still had beats bouncing in his head the next morning when he stirred, and quickly realised he was lying in water with an incoming tide. Sitting up, he looked around to see a Military Police Officer from the ship yelling at Bulldog, who was refusing to gain consciousness.

"Get up," yelled the MP while she kicked sand in Bulldog's face.

Bulldog finally came to and looked at Derrick confused.

"Derrick, get out of the water," the MP said as she glanced over.

"What's going on?" Derrick said, still feeling drunk.

"A sailor is missing and we're tracing his last steps. Did you see Able Seaman Jeffries last night?" She presented Derrick with a photograph.

"Nooo … Officer," Derrick replied. "But I did see him at the start of the night. He was going to get tattoos and girls."

"Where?"

"Barrio Barretto, I think?"

"We're in Barrio Barretto!" shouted the MP. "For fuck's sake, clean yourselves up, and get the Russian from behind the bar." She stormed off.

The Digger net lit with speculation; with most concluding that the terrorist group Abu Sayyaf had conducted a kidnap for ransom operation right under the task group's nose. Derrick sobered up to the situation and was filthy with himself, swearing that he should have seen this coming.

If something happens to Jeffries, I'll never forgive myself. I gave the situation report and the CO released us ashore.

Derrick left Bulldog and the Russian at the beach and began to make his way back to the ship when the duty officer called.

"Derrick the CO wants you back at the ship immediately. I'll collect you from the gangway."

Derrick thought of the Palestinian boy, whose parents would never see him again.

We're going to find Jeffries and get him back to his parents.

CHAPTER 10

One of the girls from the hotel gave him a lift back to his ship and when he got off the back of the motorcycle he found the duty officer waiting, looking appalled.

"You're disgusting," she said.

"I can explain," said Derrick.

"Save it for the CO. He wants you now."

The duty officer took him to a secure compartment where the CO stood staring at a map of the Philippine archipelago. The Navigator was providing a briefing on the likely sea lanes a small but fast-moving watercraft could use.

"It would be a risky move to travel on the open ocean in a small vessel during sea state six," the Navigator said.

"We didn't see any watercraft move in or out of our vicinity last night, did we Nav?" asked the CO.

"No, Sir," the Navigator replied.

"Derrick, you briefed that a kidnapping was unlikely, didn't you? Why was that?"

"Sir, recent kidnappings have all happened on small yachts sailing within the archipelago — less than 12 miles from shore. Armed attackers in fast watercraft board the yachts and capture the crew. A situation we were unlikely to encounter, Sir."

"And yet we are missing one of our own," said the CO.

"The threat from land-based kidnappings in the north of the Philippines was also low, if we were down south in Mindanao it might be a different story," Derrick continued.

"Derrick, I agree with you, and let's hope this turns out to be misadventure rather than anything sinister. I've got a feeling Able Seaman Jeffries is being held, not for ransom as we might think, but for hats and t-shirts. Make some enquiries with our friends at the police station and take gifts. Go and get my goddamn sailor back."

The local police unit was known to be very capable, but only when their palms had been sufficiently greased, and Derrick was ready to bargain. He placed the phone call.

"Captain Gabriel, my name's Derrick from Australian Task Group 455, we arrived in port last night."

"Ah yes, Mr Derrick, I hear you have lost a sailor," Captain Gabriel said with a hint of sarcasm. "Your Military Police are working with us to relocate him. Mr Derrick, we will find your sailor. We believe we know who has taken him, but it will take time and negotiating to get him back."

"Thank you, Captain Gabriel, and we appreciate your efforts. I have something for you, a token of our appreciation," said Derrick.

"I see," said Captain Gabriel, who sounded interested. "Come and see me at headquarters, Mr Derrick. It would be my honour to welcome you to the Philippines."

Derrick ended the call, but his phone immediately began vibrating with an unknown number displayed on the screen. "Hello," he answered.

"Derrick, I've got your boy," said an American accent. "He spent a night in the cells to sober up after a local gang saw him walk out of a club and pass out in a park. They took his wallet and ID, then told police he'd assaulted one of the girls from the club."

"Who is this?" Derrick asked.

"I'm your man on the ground here. I get shit done and that's all you need to know … Now listen, we need money, not a lot but enough. The gang needs to be paid, so they keep talking to us, and so do the cops — they housed Jeffries for the night, and they're not in the hotel business."

"This is a racket," said Derrick.

"Welcome to the Philippines, my man. It's a paradise until you come unstuck. Bring five hundred dollars US to the Police headquarters, a hat for Captain Gabriel and perhaps a bottle of your CO's rum. Oh, and Derrick, wish the CO all the best from the Grease Monkey, he'll know what you're talking about."

All of a sudden, a switch flicked in Derrick's mind and he realised he was being schooled in real-world international relations, the kind you don't get from writing essays and listening to lecturers preach from the safety of their classrooms. *I bet the CO was once in Able Seaman Jeffries' place,* he mused.

The aide-de-camp was standing in front of the CO's cabin as Derrick approached.

"He's not taking visitors at the moment, Derrick."

"Able Seaman Jeffries has been found."

Suddenly, the cabin door flew open. "How much does that scum bag want?" barked the CO.

"Five hundred, a hat and your rum, Sir. And the Grease Monkey says hello."

The CO regained his composure and looked deep into Derrick's soul. "Go and get Able Seaman Jeffries, have the Coxswain charge him for prejudicial conduct and then bring the paperwork and Jeffries to my office."

Derrick arrived at Police Headquarters and an escort showed him to Captain Gabriel's office.

"Take my liver and kill me!" said a fictitiously shrill voice through the thin wall followed by screams of laughter.

"Say it again, say it again," another voice said behind the wall trying to get a breath in.

"We're sure as hell not gonna take your liver, son! You're as drunk as a three-wheel shopping trolly," an American accent boomed. Shrieks of laughter echoed down the hall and Derrick wondered if it was Jeffries they were laughing about.

Derrick's escort knocked three times on the captain's door and the screams became a dull roar.

"A three-wheel shopping trolley… Ahaaa."

"Come in," said a voice behind the door and the escort pushed it open. An overweight police officer stood behind his desk and wiped the sweat from his brow.

"Derrick, is it? I am Captain Gabriel — Welcome to the Philippines, and please excuse the noise. We were just laughing about old times."

The captain stood surrounded by Naval head-dresses from across the world and he caught a glimpse of what Derrick had brought with him.

"You've bought me a hat," said Captain Gabriel grinning from ear to ear. "Thank you, Mr Derrick, I will hang it as a token of our nations' friendly bilateral relations. Please … Let me introduce you to the American, he's been waiting to meet you. I believe you have something for him also, yes?

"How's your boss, Derrick?" asked the American.

"He sends his regards, Sir, and he wanted you to have this." Derrick presented to him a bottle of rum and an unopened letter.

"Well, thank you, be sure to pass on my thanks. Let's go and see if your friend is awake. He was mighty tired and confused when he woke this morning."

Captain Gabriel and the American walked down to the cells and released Able Seaman Jeffries, who looked like he had fallen in the ocean.

"Why's he soaking wet?" asked Derrick.

"He wouldn't wake up, so we hosed him," said Captain Gabriel.

"You're a lucky man, Jeffries," said the American. "The woman you assaulted at the club last night has dropped the charges."

"Assaulted?" said Jeffries. "But …"

"Be quiet, Jeffries," Derrick interjected. "The CO wants you back on the ship immediately, and I am taking you now. Gents, I'm sorry for taking up your time and resources. But thank you for your assistance, we'll get out of your hair."

Captain Gabriel put Jeffries in the back of a police car and Derrick jumped in the other side.

"I'll see you again, Derrick," said the American with a smile, and he tapped on the roof of the car in a signal to the driver to return to the ship.

"I didn't assault anybody," said Jeffries with a quivering lip.

"I know, mate."

"The CO's going to send me home, isn't he Derrick?"

"Let's wait and see, mate."

They arrived at the ship where the Coxswain was waiting, and he marched Jeffries up the gangway and promptly charged him. Derrick then walked with Jeffries to the CO's cabin where he was waiting with the ship's Warrant Officer.

"Able Seaman Jeffries, stand to attention while the CO addresses you," said the SWO.

"Shut the door, Derrick," The CO said.

"AB Jeffries, I know you didn't assault anyone last night, but you let yourself get compromised. Drunk, you left a club alone and fell asleep in a park. You're incredibly lucky we have friends in this part of the world, and you were sold to the police and not terrorists."

"Yes, Sir," said Jeffries.

"I'm taking your shore leave from you for the rest of the trip. You can reflect on your misadventure and serve as a warning to others," said the CO.

"Yes, Sir."

"SWO, see that the charge is thrown out and assist AB Jeffries to call his parents to reassure them he is alive and well. Derrick, remain behind, will you." The SWO then took Jeffries from the cabin while Derrick moved in front of the CO and stood to attention.

"Relax, Derrick," said the CO.

"We conduct international engagement for many reasons, and this is one. See that the quarterdeck gossips play this incident down, will you. A drunk sailor is all. The Philippines won't make a deal of it, it's not in their interest and they're used to it."

"Yes, Sir."

"Derrick, twenty years ago the American 'Grease Monkey', got me out of trouble when I was young and dumb … and as much as it pains me to think of sailors still fucking up in foreign ports, they do, and well-placed agents like 'Grease Monkey' continue to clean up the mess. We need friends; they lubricate the fractured world through diplomacy and favour … but one day our friends will ask for payment."

Derrick left the CO's cabin and went to the quarterdeck to get some air and check his phone. When he opened the rear door the evening darkness blinded him, and he fumbled for his phone to see. He stood dead still to avoid falling overboard and his eyes locked on to the screen.

I made it into the State Tennis semi-final, read Charlie's message. *It's in a month, will you be in Sydney then?*

Hey, yeah, I should be back then. I'll call you tomorrow, it'd be nice to talk.

Derrick's eyes regained their focus, and he watched squid chasing bait in the moonlight. His mind raced as he tried to process the last 24 hours, and he found it hard to control his thoughts and elevating heart rate. He took some slow, deep breaths, and began to think through the end of year trip.

I'm getting back in the ocean, where the 'real world' doesn't exist.

CHAPTER 11

Derrick returned from Southeast Asia but before he and Charlie spent the Christmas break island-hopping through the Pacific, he donned a green visor and sweatbands and watched her play tennis in the State semi-final.

"You look amazing," he said after Charlie had dressed and was ready to play.

"Thanks, my sponsor sent it to me … the skirt's too short, but let's see how I go," she said with a wink.

A small crowd assembled when Charlie took to the court, and she glided effortlessly across it to win her first set. Foolishly, Derrick was surprised at how well she played, and he stared at her beauty like a fawning teenager.

"Wow, she's unbelievable," said a man standing nearby and Derrick immediately became jealous.

The first two sets had been a gift and Charlie was well placed to take the third when her opponent sent the ball high in the air and Derrick looked on hoping for victory. As Charlie turned to race back to the base line, she pivoted on the ball of her foot, but her knee gave way and she collapsed to the floor.

"Charlie!" Derrick yelled from the crowd.

Charlie straightened her knee, put her hand in the air to say, 'I'm okay,' and hobbled to the baseline ready to return serve.

The opponent tossed the ball and served with thunderous pace in attempt to take back the game and set. Charlie took one pace to the ball and sent the ball along the sideline deep to the back of the court.

"Game, set and match," said the umpire and the crowd clapped and cheered. Derrick ran over to congratulate her.

"That was intense, are you okay?"

"I'll be fine, let's go to the islands," said Charlie.

Derrick's last deployment was valuable in many ways, but his insight into realpolitik now meant less time in bars and more with Charlie — a win-win, especially in her eyes, and they managed to get through the break without a major argument.

On his return to work, Derrick received an order to sit an officer selection board. Still a Private, his mates saw the transfer to officer as the highest insult, but he knew the change would afford more opportunities and increase his chances of actual influence.

Dressed in a dark suit and anxious to mourn the passing of his career as a soldier, Derrick flew to Canberra where the bitter cold reminded him of London with Dingo. In nervous anticipation of what was to come, he arrived at Army headquarters and mingled with the other officer candidates. Derrick was used to briefing senior officers regularly, but this time anxiety consumed his mind.

"So, what do you do?" he asked one of the candidates, in an attempt to soothe his mind.

"I'm a vet," said the woman.

"Oh, where have you been?" said Derrick.

"Not a veteran, I'm a veterinarian at Australia Zoo."

"We have vets in the military?" Derrick asked.

"Of course! Who looks after the dogs?" she replied with a smile.

An Army Psychologist welcomed them to Canberra, and immediately directed them onto a bus where they were driven to the Royal Military College, Duntroon. They arrived a few minutes later, and a sprightly young personal training instructor in small red shorts and a tight white t-shirt bounded onto the bus and told them to get off.

"Right, good morning. Get off the bus and line up in front of it," said the Corporal with impressive quadriceps. "Ready. Go."

Once the officer candidates were lined up the Corporal gave further detail. "The change room is to my left, your right, and I want you changed and ready to complete your initial fitness assessment before we move on with the rest of the day's activities. You've got three minutes!"

The Corporal PTI blew his whistle, and the candidates ran to the change rooms.

"That started quick," said one of the candidates as they threw freshly pressed suits across the change rooms and furiously changed.

"You watch, they'll tell us we're too slow and to get back in our suits," said Derrick.

"Yeah, next we'll be playing get in your bed, get out of your bed," the candidate replied with a laugh.

"Ex AJ?" asked Derrick.

"Yeah, ex-infantry getting back in as a Legal Officer," said the candidate. They emerged from the change rooms and lined up in front of the bus. Derrick stood in disbelief when no one barked orders at them or told them they weren't quick enough.

"Good work, everyone. We'll now complete your fitness assessment before working through a series of activities to see how you work as a team," said the Corporal, and he walked them over to the gymnasium.

"Good work? We've only just put our shorts on," whispered Derrick, certain of a ruse.

"Mate, this is entry to officer life," said the prospective Legal Officer. "They're not going to smash us here."

The morning was a mix of a fitness test, impossible tasks and written work, with the afternoon consisting of a series of discussions that culminated with a senior officer interview. Derrick felt like he had performed well but there was one thing left hanging over his head.

"Cut the shit, Derrick," said an Infantry Lieutenant Colonel. "You're a serving member; tell me what happened with your DUI?"

"I was drunk, and made a really poor decision, Sir, and it nearly cost me my career," said Derrick, knowing full well this would be the first question.

"Yes, but did you learn from it?" the Lieutenant Colonel enquired further.

"It changed my life, Sir, and I've tried to do everything I can to better myself ever since."

The panel continued to interrogate his history and expose his poor life choices. But, with a steely gaze Derrick responded to the probing panel like his life depended on it. Finally, he sat exhausted and the Lieutenant Colonel told him to wait outside while they deliberated on the outcome.

Derrick waited for what seemed like an hour before the Psychologist told to him to return.

"Sit down," said the Lieutenant Colonel.

"Today you've been successful, and it's recommended that you commission as an officer in the Australian Army. Congratulations, Derrick, you got your transfer."

Derrick felt compelled to hug the Infantry Officer but sensed it wasn't the right time, so he thanked the panel and made a rapid withdrawal in case they changed their minds.

A cab was waiting outside when he left Army headquarters and he opened the door and jumped into the backseat.

"To the airport," said Derrick before he noticed a neatly dressed woman in sunglasses in the front seat.

"Oh, I'm sorry," said Derrick. "I should have realised the cab wasn't available."

"It's okay, I'm going to the airport too, so we can share," said the woman, looking down at her phone. "Let's go," she said calmly to the driver before glancing over at Derrick and lowering her glasses to the bridge of her nose.

"You seem very excited …" She paused, waiting for Derrick to introduce himself.

"Derrick, Ma'am, and I just commissioned as an officer."

"Oh well done you, Derrick," said the woman in a flat, almost dismissive tone as she turned back to her phone. "And what kind of officer will you be then?"

"PR, Ma'am."

"Ah okay, STRATCOMM," she said.

"And you, Ma'am?"

"Policy, with Foreign Affairs."

Derrick didn't pay much attention to the woman as he hurriedly texted Kate. *Mum, guess who's an Army officer!*

It was only a short journey from Army Headquarters to the airport and the cab quickly pulled into the terminal.

"I'll get the cab, Derrick," said the woman. "My treat."

"Awesome, thanks Ma'am." Derrick leapt out of the cab and made his way into the departure lounge.

"I knew you were going to give me good news," said Kate, having called back after receiving his message. "Your father has just stepped out, but I'll tell him the news when he gets back. He'll be thrilled."

"Thanks Mum. I'm about to board my flight home. Tell Dad I'll call him later." Peering at his watch, Derrick saw that he had just enough time for a celebratory drink at the bar while the line for boarding dwindled. He bought a beer and was sitting with a view to his waiting aircraft when the woman from the cab sat down next to him with a glass of wine.

"And where's home?" asked the woman, having caught Derrick's full attention.

"Brisbane, Ma'am," said Derrick, who was locked onto her searing grey eyes and simple beauty.

"Oh, that must be nice, with the surf and sand at your fingertips." The woman took a sip of her wine and stared into Derrick's eyes.

Not knowing where to look, Derrick filled the awkward silence. "Where are you off to, Ma'am?" he said before sipping his beer nervously, like someone who shouldn't be drinking on duty.

"Sydney, then Washington." The woman broke her gaze and relaxed in her chair. "Not nearly as nice as the Gold Coast."

"Yeah, but I'll be moving soon — down to the cold of the nation's capital."

"Ah yes, all roads lead back to Canberra. You might work with me one day, then we can enjoy the cold of Washington and Canberra."

Derrick laughed. "I'd like that, Ma'am."

"Is that your flight about to leave?"

"Shit … sorry to leave you Ma'am, but I'd better run." Derrick finished his beer and grabbed his backpack. "Nice to meet you, Ma'am." He raised his hand to shake the woman's.

"Emily, please call me Emily." She shook his hand and held it for a second longer than usual.

Flight staff then called Derrick's name over the loudspeaker, and he smiled at Emily before turning to his flight.

"Welcome back, Derrick," said the air hostess who greeted him back on board the flight to Brisbane. "I trust the trip to Canberra went well."

CHAPTER 12

Derrick arrived back in Canberra two months later, at the beginning of winter. Autumnal leaves still littered the ground, and country pubs welcomed punters with roaring log fires. Before he'd unpacked or acclimatised to the cold, his new boss pulled him in the office.

"Hope you've settled in, Derrick. We need you to take a team to Southeast Asia. Thai special forces are training a rifle company in jungle warfare." The boss handed him a deployment order and smiled. "Pack your jungle hammock mate, the bush rats are fucken huge over there."

Seventy-two hours later Derrick was on a flight bound for Bangkok, with his Sergeant. An Australian soldier in uniform picked them up at Suvarnabhumi Airport, Bangkok and they drove four hours' north, close to the border of Myanmar. It was late when they arrived at camp, and the driver showed them straight to their beds.

"This bed is concrete," said the Sergeant as she brushed through the mosquito net. "Oh my God," said the Sergeant after a couple more minutes.

"What now?" asked Derrick, already thinking the trip was going to be painful.

"My boyfriend just broke up with me. Fucking Prick," she said.

Derrick was silent for a minute, until he heard a sniff like she was crying.   "I'm sorry mate, someone else will pop up. They always do."

The Sergeant didn't reply, and they both drifted off to sleep listening to bullfrogs and humming mosquitoes gathered on the net.

They woke at dawn to the smell of spot fires and a rousing song blasting through the camp speakers.

"Is that reveille?" said Derrick, stirring from a broken night's sleep.

"Sounds like propaganda to me," said the Sergeant with a scowl.

Derrick took his camera and peered outside from his accommodation. Misty mountains filled his viewfinder, and he took his first photograph. He waved at some monks making their way to a nearby temple and watched the Thai troops jog in formation.

What a terrible start to the day, mused Derrick breathing in the thick morning air.

He met the Officer Commanding Bravo Company for breakfast who mapped out the week's events.

"The first few days are a series of meet and greet activities to get to know the Thai soldiers — expect to eat lots of Pad Thai and drink the local moonshine, it's delicious but the ethanol might kill you. Then we'll spend 48 hours in the jungle conducting survival training with Special Forces, followed by a three-day field exercise in the mountains. They're good soldiers and officers here, Derrick, their OC trained at Sandhurst. One point to mention though," said the OC followed by a short pause. "Some of the methods and techniques used here might not always align with our own, so please use discretion when capturing imagery and vision."

"Understood, Sir," said Derrick, "the moonshine won't see the light of day."

Derrick back-briefed the Sergeant, but trying to get her to engage with anything other than her messages was proving difficult. "Stop staring at your phone," he said. "There's plenty of fish ..."

"You wouldn't understand! My last relationship ended while I was in Iraq. I came back to an empty house with everything gone. We're never home long enough for anything to work out," she said, frustrated.

Derrick had his own relationship woes and had little sympathy for others, but in that moment, his heart sank as he realised that his job was just as much about supporting and managing his mates as it was about lofty strategic goals.

"Shit, sorry mate. Focus on the work, you'll meet someone when the time's right," said Derrick, before he left the Sergeant and went to join Bravo Company, who'd begun a PT session on a fog-engulfed grass oval.

"Right, three rounds, fifty push-ups — one hundred squats — a lap round the base, then twenty burpees," said Bravo Company's personal trainer instructor just as a company of Thai soldiers joined them on the oval. A Thai Lieutenant stood next to Derrick and smiled.

"Fifty push-ups — one hundred squats — run round the base, twenty burpees," shouted the Lieutenant with a heavy Thai accent and his soldiers began to laugh.

"Why are they laughing?" asked Derrick.

"The fog will lift soon, and it will be very hot," said the Lieutenant. "They don't think you can make it through the session."

The PTI overheard the conversation and chimed in, not sure if he should be nervous or not. "It's bloody hot in Australia, mate."

"We'll see how fit you are and if you have acclimatised," said the Lieutenant.

The PTI looked at his watch and drew in a deep breath. "Five, four, three, two, go," he shouted at the top of his lungs and pressed play on a Bluetooth speaker.

The soldiers immediately jumped to the ground and began doing push-ups to a cadence of ACDC's 'Thunderstruck'.

Shards of sunlight pierced through the fog half-way through the first set of squats, which revealed mountains that channelled the sun's heat on to their position. The

Thais were slender and fast, and didn't seem particularly affected by the increasing temperature, but Bravo Company, however, were 'strong like ox' and as they began the third round, the heat took its first casualties.

"STOP, STOP, STOP!" yelled the PTI, staring at two motionless soldiers on the grass. "What's wrong with you?" he asked, kneeling next to one of them.

"We're being cooked like an egg," the soldier groaned and hid his face from the sun.

"Did you drink the moonshine last night?" asked the PTI and, on cue, the soldier vomited onto the steaming grass.

"Take them to the first aid point," said the Thai Lieutenant and he pointed to some shade where a makeshift sprinkler system had been set up.

A section from Bravo Company carried the two soldiers to the sprinkler system where cooling mist lowered their core temperature and saved them from further injury.

"Mate, you just saved my ass," said the PTI to the Lieutenant who smiled and ordered his soldiers back to their unit.

"Do us a favour, Derrick, don't mention this in your story."

"Same team, bro," replied Derrick.

"Just making sure."

Derrick left Bravo company rotating shirtless through the sprinkler system like children at a theme park before he bumped into the OC walking back to his accommodation.

"We're moving to the jungle tomorrow morning at 0500," said the OC.

Derrick nodded and kept walking, wondering what the OC would make of Bravo company suffering from heat the day before a jungle exercise.

"We're going out in the field tomorrow — I'm setting my alarm for four," Derrick said to his Sergeant, who was still in bed.

"Four? Why so early?"

"The company steps off at 0500. Manage yourself, but be ready to step off five minutes before."

The next morning Derrick stood outside in the dark waiting for the Sergeant. At exactly five to five, the Sergeant emerged and they joined the rest of the company, who had sufficiently recovered from the heat.

Smoke from charcoal fires dissipated beneath the canopy and the first cracks of light appeared through the shadows. Thai Special Forces led the company to a clearing where they had set some traps overnight. Two chickens had been caught, both with a noose around their necks. The birds panicked when they saw the soldiers but trying to fly away only tightened the noose.

The Thai soldiers demonstrated how to construct a variety of traps and by breakfast the Australians had set their own. They patrolled through the jungle collecting fruit and water, and then laid out a defensive position. The Australians watched on as Thai soldiers set trip wires that initiated early warning attack devices made from bamboo. The sound of knocking bamboo rang out eerily across the jungle and set the scene of what was to come.

In the afternoon, Derrick noticed the smoke had started to thicken again. Thinking that there would be a barbeque soon, he turned around, expecting to see his Sergeant but found he was standing by himself.

A bird whistle from the clearing rang out and the Thai soldiers motioned for him to come quietly.

The Sergeant was filming quietly while the Thai Lieutenant from yesterday's PT session held a long trap made of reeds.

"What's in there?" Derrick mouthed to the Sergeant.

"He caught something from the river …"

The soldiers gathered in a half-circle around the Lieutenant as he shook the trap.

"Be careful," said the Lieutenant. "Don't come to close." He then opened the rear hatch and a large, black king cobra dropped to the floor. The snake reared up in front of the crowd and they edged back in panic.

"Snake is good to eat for food and to drink its blood for hydration," said the calm and collected Lieutenant. He took the snake by the tail then pinned its head with a fork from a branch.

"Remove the head to kill it, or poison will pump through the body, and you will die when you eat." He raised a machete from his side and swiftly delivered a blow behind the snake's head.

"Then you drink." He held the snake high and drank the blood before sharing it with the Australian soldiers.

"Give me some!" yelled the Sergeant with an apparent rush of blood to the head. She knelt in front of the crowd and the Thai Lieutenant milked the snake's blood above her. The crowd roared as she drank and smeared blood across her face like she'd conquered a demon. She seemed to be on some sort of primal high, and gained newfound admiration from Bravo Company.

Derrick captured on camera the Sergeant regaining her drive, to prove hard times do get better. *A primal connection was the perfect antidote for heartbreak.*

Bravo Company continued in the Thai jungle for the rest of the week, avoiding direct sunlight and concentrating on survival techniques. Derrick had what he needed for a media package after a couple of days and decided to leave Bravo Company to train without a camera in their face.

On the drive back to Bangkok he reviewed the footage and checked his emails to see that his boss had been trying to get in touch.

"FFS Derrick where are you? Send through your product immediately. Foreign Affairs need it ASAP," read an email from his boss in Canberra.

Foreign Affairs, what do they want with Bravo Company's jungle training?
Derrick and his Sergeant prepared a video news release and article and sent it back to Canberra.

They boarded their flight and by the time they had reached Sydney an article in the Bangkok Post read 'More than just an Aussie holiday destination — Militaries deepen ties in Jungle.'

Back in Sydney, Derrick Stayed with Charlie for a few days, but it wasn't the homecoming he expected. She told him about the tennis tournaments he'd been missing and the other guys that kept asking her out.

"When are you getting out, Derrick?" Charlie asked. "Are you ever going to stay longer than a few days? Fuck, I'm sick of this Army shit!"

CHAPTER 13

Derrick returned to Canberra deflated, and no amount of relationship advice was going to help his predicament. His long-distance relationship with Charlie wasn't working, but for the moment the status quo remained. Bulldog had just transferred to the unit as a Photographer and Derrick couldn't wait to get back to work.

"Bulldog, how are ya?" said Derrick, spotting him in the carpark on his first day.

"Good to see you, mate! Saw you were in Thailand recently? Get up to much mischief with those ladyboys?" said Bulldog with a laugh.

It had been over a year since he and Bulldog were last at sea, and he was looking forward to deploying with him again.

"I know you've only just got to Canberra, but after you've settled in, we're sailing to Asia from Perth. First port Sri Lanka," said Derrick.

"Sri Lanka?"

"Since the 2004 tsunami a Sri Lankan counter terrorism unit that fought the Tamil Tigers during the Thirty-Year War is now trained in disaster response too. We're going to work with them."

"What's the messaging?" asked Bulldog.

"That we're mates, and we have more things in common than just cricket and curry."

Politicians in Canberra were keen on demonstrating that Australia was a player in the Indian Ocean as well as the Pacific. It was a strategic shift from the 'forever wars' in the Middle East, to something a little closer to home.

The Task Group sailed from Perth with a powerful southern swell pushing towards Indonesia. They stopped at the Cocos-Keeling Islands to reinforce Australia's commitment to its territories, and after 10 days at sea arrived in Colombo, Sri Lanka.

"Derrick!" yelled Bulldog, flinging open the door to his compartment. "Don't release the video of Frank."

Frank was an Australian sailor who was born in Sri Lanka, and Derrick had spent the journey so far producing a 'home coming' style media clip, using him as the hero.

"Frank spoke to his sister, who said not to get his name in the media," said Bulldog. "He doesn't want them sniffing round his family."

"Shit," said Derrick. "That was our ice breaker; I'll have a talk to him."

Derrick spoke to Frank and reassured him that as the face of Sri Lankan – Australian relations, he was bringing the countries closer together. He had carefully crafted Frank's image to represent the brotherhood of both Commonwealth countries, and once Frank saw the finished product, he was more than happy to promote the strategic exchange.

That night, local dignitaries attended a reception on the Australian ship's quarterdeck and vision of 'Frank returning home' was shown on arrival. The military and political elite sipped cocktails and nibbled on canapés while Derrick watched on from afar.

"This kind of thing makes me sick," said Bulldog as he sipped on a wine.

"Yeah, but look at your work — Frank's being shone onto the side of a ship. Let's go get a beer in town," said Derrick with a laugh.

They walked off the wharf and took a bus to the Dutch Hospital. On route the bus stopped at the fancy hotels surrounding Colombo Fort, and picked up some of the crew whose invite to the ship's reception was lost in the mail. Derrick was annoyed at himself for not booking a hotel for the visit. *But think of the dollars you'll save,* he said to himself.

"Is this place really a hospital?" Bulldog asked, gagging for a beer.

"When the Dutch East Indies Company ruled the waves. Now there are bars everywhere," said Derrick.

"Well, I'm parched and could do with a drink," said Bulldog.

The boys picked up from where they'd left off on their last deployment and reminisced of getting drunk in foreign ports, while slowly getting drunk in a foreign port.

"I'm gonna have a goat curry," said Derrick after his fourth pint.

"No, let's get the chilli crab," said Bulldog pushing Derrick off his stool towards the Ministry of Crab restaurant. The two of them play-wrestled out the front before pretending to be sober and walking in to eat.

Like a couple of drunk disciples, Derrick and Bulldog returned to the ship to sleep off the booze and crab. But as the ship gently rocked so did Derrick's stomach, and he lurched out of bed and ran to the bathroom to throw up in the bin. He'd read in the ship's joining instructions not to throw up in the toilets because the negative air pressure could cause him to pass out, so he crept into the shower and pulled the bin in behind the curtain.

"Dear God, if you help me tonight … I won't eat seafood and I'll work really hard," Derrick prayed. "Apart from fish, I'll eat fish, I know you like them."

Bulldog burst in two minutes later, wrapped his arms round the toilet bowl and roared like a lion.

"I'm sick," said Bulldog once he caught his breath back.

"Me too," Derrick whimpered back.

They both fell asleep where they sat, until the late-night revellers woke them up when they came through the bathroom. No-one was any the wiser when they left the cubicle and shower. The next day, it was all but a memory.

Small but idyllic waves crashed onto palm-fringed beaches the next morning and Derrick and Bulldog decided to go surfing. They drove down the coast where the water was clear and blue, and drank milk from coconuts from the roadside to rehydrate from the previous night's misadventure. They hired a couple of boards from a local surf school and paddled around for an hour.

When Derrick got out, he saw that his phone had been ringing hot.

Limit your movement, and stay away from tourist hotspots, said one of his messages.

"Have you seen this?" said Bulldog, pointing at his phone.

Derrick called the Task Group Watch Keeper to see what was going on.

"G'day Watch, it's Derrick. Have you been trying to get me?"

"Make your way back to the ship, we've got intel there's a threat. The Commander's recalled the Task Group for a clear lower deck this afternoon and we've upped security. Stay away from markets and crowds, mate."

Derrick and Bulldog meandered their way along the Sri Lankan coastline until they hit the heaving traffic of Colombo.

"Stay away from markets?" said Derrick. "Everywhere is a fucking market and we're two white guys in a 4WD."

"Mate, no one's going to randomly target us now, just relax," said Bulldog with his seat back, window down and feet out the window.

Children with smiling faces waved the 4WD through the bustling streets to the wharf where the Australian Task Group sat surrounded by Chinese container ships. A crowd had formed on the light vehicle deck when Derrick walked back onboard the ship, and minutes later the Commander addressed the crowd.

"Listen in … I don't want to destroy your leave plans but the threat has increased with our presence here. Islamic State sympathisers are looking for soft targets, and we're not going to present one. Let the terror attacks seen across the world serve as a reminder to keep alert."

The Commander gave a list of arbitrary dos and don'ts then dismissed the crowd.

"We got called back for that?" grumbled an irritated Bulldog before heading to his bed.

Derrick was keen to spend the last of his day off with a beer in hand watching the sunset and decided to ignore the Commander's advice and go back to the Dutch Hospital. He signed off the ship and bounced down the gangway to where an elegantly dressed woman in a suit stopped him at the bottom.

"Derrick, is it? I'm Emily Carter from Foreign Affairs." She extended a hand to shake his. As he gripped her hand and stared into her grey eyes, he knew they'd met before, but couldn't remember where or when.

"We're going to the Sunken Village tomorrow and I hear you're coming along?"

"Yeah, we're capturing a disaster relief exercise," said Derrick.

"Great, I'm interested in pushing the engagement to local media and hoping you can give us what you shoot. I'll introduce you to the disaster response team; they'll get you the vision you need."

"Oh okay, perfect," said Derrick, surprised that diplomats had such good relationships with the military.

Emily smiled. "See you tomorrow then, Derrick." She got into a blacked-out SUV and her driver gently pulled away from the wharf.

I swear I've met her before…

The late afternoon sun was starting to fade, and the surrounding buildings and ships began to cast long shadows. He walked along the checker-plate landscape to the Dutch Hospital, where he sipped a beer and thought of those familiar grey eyes that he knew he had seen before.

CHAPTER 14

It was still dark when the Commander of the Counter Terrorism Unit pulled up next to the gangway. The Commander wore golden aviators and had a rock star demeanour when Derrick opened the front passenger door to the SUV and sat next to him.

"Derrick, pleased to meet you, baby," said the Commander.

Emily sat in the back seat working on her phone. She groaned when Bulldog bounced in next to her.

"Morning all!" Bulldog said loudly.

The Commander turned to his new passengers. "To the Sunken Village," he said like Harrison Ford from an Indiana Jones movie before speeding off through the early morning Colombo traffic.

"Since the Tsunami we train in disaster response, we owe that to the people," the Commander said while negotiating the tuk-tuks and street vendors. "But during the war we fought Tamil Tiger terrorism. I've watched trees move inch by inch as terrorists hid inside waiting to kill us. Now we're fighting the Islamic State, and we will kill them just like we did the Tamil Terrorists."

They drove for hours while the Commander told war stories, before finally pulling off the main highway onto an embankment, where a zodiac inflatable boat was waiting in the mangroves. Two Australian soldiers got out and offered a hand to Emily.

"Can we help you down, Ma'am?" said one of the soldiers, and Emily took their hands and stepped in the boat.

Derrick didn't think to question why the Australian soldiers were there and got in with Bulldog, followed by the Sri Lankan Commander. They slowly motored along a winding channel to a wooden boatshed masked by a mangrove forest deep within the estuary.

From above, the boatshed resembled a mangrove canopy, and from the channel a natural arch formed where a wooden ramp led from the water. *Presumably to enable zodiacs to launch and recover from inside* thought Derrick. A raised boardwalk surrounded the boatshed and seemed to lead deeper into the forest, but Derrick couldn't see beyond the first turn.

Derrick looked at Emily. "This channel seems deep?"

"We built it," Emily replied. "We've been working here for months."

"Built it?" Confused, he watched Bulldog filming a dark green speedboat approaching. Bigger than the zodiac, the speedboat slowly idled towards them, with an Australian soldier standing behind a .50 calibre machine gun mounted to the deck.

"I thought we were watching a disaster response exercise?" said Derrick.

"We'll drop you at that later. Right now, we need to send a strong message to Sri Lanka's enemies," said Emily.

A third boat with Sri Lankan soldiers on board followed the green speedboat and the Commander pointed at Bulldog. "Please … get on."

Bulldog jumped on the boat and sat behind the gunner.

Emily held Derrick back and waved the boats off. "Come with me," she said.

They walked along the boardwalk through the mangroves, to an isolated beach where a man was fishing on a bamboo stilt as gentle waves trickled beneath him.

"The people are kept poor by corruption," said Emily. "They suffered through a horrific war and now terrorists and corrupt officials are intent on control."

The man motioned to Derrick to join him on a nearby bamboo pole.

"Go on," encouraged Emily.

Derrick waded through the bubbling surf and sat on top of an ocean perch. Children chased small sharks in the shallows and curious villagers joined Emily on the beach while Derrick snapped pictures of the beautiful scenery from his ocean mount.

An hour later, Derrick got down from the perch and found that the villagers had set up lunch under palm trees fringing the beach. Sipping from a coconut, Emily looked over her sunglasses at him as he approached.

"Should we find Bulldog?" asked Derrick. "We've been gone for ages."

"They'll be back in half an hour. Try the coconuts, they're delicious."

When they finally walked back along the boardwalk from the beach, Bulldog was waiting at the boatshed.

"Derrick, the footage is incredible — these guys just lit up an island," said Bulldog.

"Thank you, Bulldog," said Emily curtly. "I trust you'll both abide by the 'need to know' principle." She looked at one of the Australian soldiers who had helped her get in the boat earlier. "Take the zodiac and get Derrick and Bulldog to the disaster response demonstration so they can capture it for the news networks. Also make sure they get the Task Group bus back to the ship. We can't have them left behind."

The soldier zipped them along the waterways in the zodiac, and slowed down as the activity of the demonstration came into view up ahead. The demonstration was being conducted in the middle of an estuary, and the soldier took a wide berth and edged their boat in among the others.

Focusing, Derrick realised that the Sri Lankan Commander was narrating a mock rescue of a pregnant woman stuck on the roof of a flooded house. The rest of the Task Group were in boats like their zodiac, so they didn't stand out and no-one knew they'd been missing. Bulldog began recording and, over the course of the afternoon, put together a video news release demonstrating the closeness of Australia and Sri Lanka.

Before the visitors were to be returned to their ship the Commander asked them to take a moment to meditate at the top of a hill that looked out over the ocean. The Commander walked next to Derrick and guided him to the top of the hill.

"You have been a great help to the People of Sri Lanka today. We cannot give in to greed and corruption. We'll show the assholes that they won't win."

Derrick rested against a tree, faced the ocean and closed his eyes. *What the fuck is going on?*

Emily walked up next to him while he had his eyes shut and gently ruined the serenity. "Jumping on the bus?" she said softly.

"I didn't want to go back with you anyway …" said Derrick with a wry smile.

"A small favour? Can I have the memory cards from the camera? I'll make sure you have what you need for the news networks later."

Derrick pulled his hand from his pocket and put the cards in Emily's palm. "Here, I never thought I'd return to the ship with them."

"I'll see you get them back … You've made some friends today, and you never know when you might need to call on them."

He watched Emily walk back down the hill, get in the SUV and roll off into the night. Soon, he and Bulldog followed and got on the bus with the others from the Task

Group. After a long journey back, they arrived at the ship at midnight, and a familiar looking man in a suit handed Derrick an envelope as he approached the gangway.

"Open it in the ship, mate," said the man.

Once inside his cabin, Derrick opened the envelope and tipped two memory cards into his palm. He also pulled out a note: *Vision sent to local media.*

Derrick inserted the cards into a reader attached to his computer but could see they had been wiped. His mind racing, he lay down in bed to piece the last 24 hours together. He drifted in and out of consciousness with whirling images of children playing in shallows, friendly fishermen smiling, small boats with massive combat power — and Emily.

In the morning he woke to the sound of his phone vibrating. *Good work, Derrick*, flashed up on his phone and the headlines of the day read: *Tsunami of hope, Australia & Sri Lanka bond through disaster relief exercise.*

As he scrolled through his phone, he noticed Emily had sent a message in the early hours of the morning:

Meet me at the Colonial Hotel at 2pm and wear a suit.

When he arrived that afternoon, the waiters were handing out champagne and cocktails, but he stood at the bar and ordered a beer.

Emily was busy chatting amongst the crowd but when she saw him, she broke out of her conversation and walked to the bar. "Quite the headline this morning," she said. "The product was amazing, please thank … Bulldog, was it?"

The barman placed a cold beer on top of the bar, which Derrick took and turned to look out at the ocean.

"What's going on, Ma'am? Are we helping the military overthrow a government?"

Without replying, Emily walked outside onto a deck overlooking the ocean, her fitted black dress showing off her incredible figure so much that Derrick couldn't help but stare. He followed her outside where the gentle breeze ruffled her blonde hair and her grey eyes offset the turquoise ocean.

"The security situation in Sri Lanka is deteriorating," said Emily, turning to face him. "Hard-line Buddhists are blaming Middle Eastern Influences for creating a more conservative and insular Muslim population. The rhetoric around Muslims and the rise of Islamic State has created a tinderbox that's set to explode. No-one here wants another war. You've seen it for yourself, and the support we provide assists with stabilising the region. We're here to help, Derrick …"

Emily briefly put a hand on his shoulder and then left him on the deck to go and greet more guests. Unwilling to make small talk with dignitaries, and having gotten the answer he came for, he helped himself to a prawn cocktail then caught a cab back to the ship. As the cab drove him back along the palm-fringed coast a news alert flashed up on his phone.

Muslims Down Shutters as Hard-liners Attack, read the headline.

"Shit, she's right," he whispered.

Derrick arrived back at the ship, and they set sail for India during the period of darkness, wargames with India beckoned. But as the ship steamed across the Bay of Bengal, Derrick received an untitled email marked urgent from Emily. He opened the mail and scrolled down …

They attacked in the morning while the devout were at Easter Mass. Holidaymakers were having breakfast in their hotels while six suicide bombers detonated their devices. Three churches and three hotels were destroyed leaving 267 dead and hundreds more injured.

CHAPTER 15

News of the terrorist attack in Sri Lanka had stolen the enthusiasm of the Task Group, with many of the soldiers and sailors having met some of those who perished. Derrick was devasted to find out that a six-year-old girl who attended the afternoon soiree at the Colonial Hotel had died while attending Easter Mass with her father.

Emily, I'm terribly sorry to hear of the tragic events that unfolded since our Task Group left Sri Lanka. I'm sorry I couldn't have been of more help to you and the people there. I trust our friends will help find those responsible – Derrick.

Over the next couple of days, the geopolitical jigsaw in Derrick's mind slowly pieced together, and his hunger for information and context kept him awake at night. As the Task Group steamed into India, he was determined to do more to shape opinion, and he spent the time at sea researching why they were in India, and why now.

It didn't take him long to find out that successive Australian Governments had been trying to restore the U.S., Japan, India and Australia Quadrilateral Security Dialogue that then Australian Prime Minister Kevin Rudd withdrew from in 2008. As part of this restoration, Derrick and the Task Group were now on their way to India for an Exercise to thaw the military frost.

A harbour pilot guided the Australian warship past piles of steaming potash before docking at an east coast Naval base. They arrived without the usual fanfare that accompanies visits like this, and Derrick was surprised no-one with rank was there to greet them. An Australian submarine was also alongside, and the boat's Captain was welcomed on board the Frigate.

"They'll keep us waiting," said the Captain, frustration all over his face. "They're still angry at us for leaving the Quad and want to show us we're not important."

Derrick needed to capture vision of a warm Indian greeting before he could step off the ship, and he also needed to get to the iron ore terminal where *HMAS Charleston* was coming in to port. He felt it was down to him to tell the world the Quad was back on track, and he wasn't going to ruin his chance.

Bulldog looked over as a group of Indian Navy guards marshalled a group of dock workers from the port. "Looks like they're closing the facility," he said. "They're clearing everyone off the terminal."

"I'm sure it's just to limit access to our ships. The brass has probably realised we're here and scared their staff into action," said Derrick.

The guards ushered the workers outside an iron gate that also kept the Australians sealed off from India. A fast-moving van approached the gate blasting its horn and the driver, an Australian sailor, gestured wildly to the guards to let him through. Derrick recognised the sailor from Sri Lanka and watched as, after he produced some paperwork, they let him through and he parked next to the ship.

The sailor saluted the ship as he walked on board and promptly made his way over to Derrick and Bulldog, who had their camera equipment set up.

"The Base Commander will be here soon," said the sailor. "Australia hardly blips on their radar in a country of over a billion. I'm also taking you to the iron-ore terminal once we're done, so give us a wink when we can go."

Two Indian Navy captains approached the Frigate at a brisk walk and stood at the bottom of the gangway.

"Permission to come aboard?" one of the captains asked.

A Boatswain piped the Indian Officers aboard, and the Task Group Commander greeted them on the quarterdeck.

"Welcome to Australia, gentlemen," he said, brimming with energy.

"Welcome to India," replied the officers and they exchanged handshakes and friendly smiles. "The Admiral sends his apologies for being unable to meet you. He had to attend a political engagement. He's very much looking forward to your reception next week, after the exercise."

Bulldog looked at Derrick and the sailor with a wink. He'd got the shot that said the Indian – Australian relationship was back on track, and now they had to get off the ship. The three of them slipped down the gangway while the military officials spoke, and got into the sailor's van.

"Anyone else coming?" asked the sailor.

"No, let's go... We've got to shoot the *Charleston* coming in," said Derrick.

"Easy," said the sailor. "Just a quick detour via the hotel, the curry here is keeping me regular as clockwork."

As the van approached the iron gate, a guard motioned for the driver to wind down the window. "Papers and ID?" asked the guard.

The sailor pulled out a manila folder stamped with 'Australian High Commission' and showed him the contents.

"Them in the back?" the guard asked.

"They came with me … Boys show them your ID," said the sailor.

"No-one is leaving tonight, customs want to inspect the ship," the guard interjected.

"We've got to get back, its urgent," tap-danced the sailor.

The Indian officer walked from the van into the customs office and disappeared inside. He reappeared with an angry Navy Captain, who stormed over.

"Nobody is getting on or off this ship without me knowing," said the Captain with his elbow on the van's window.

"We just came to greet the ship, Sir," said the sailor. "We'll return to our hotel and come back tomorrow."

The Captain stared at the sailor, then glanced at the Derrick and Bulldog in the back. Derrick swallowed nervously when the man grasped the whistle hanging around his neck and blew a shrill burst while raising his left hand. The Australians sat tensely as the gate slowly opened and the Captain waved them through a crowd of workers that prevented a clear path out.

"Great, so we're illegal aliens in India," said Bulldog as the van bounced down the potholed road.

"The guard was doing us a favour, he knew what we were up to," Derrick reassured him.

"Yeah, the rules are loose round here, aye," shouted the sailor from the front, looking happy with the outcome of his lies.

When they arrived at the container terminal, bulk carrier ships were being filled with iron ore pellets from conveyor belts. Red dust filled the air and as they waited for the *Charleston* to dock, their uniforms became the colour of rust.

"G'day mate! What're you doing here?" shouted an Indian man with a quasi-Aussie accent, who was monitoring the conveyor belts.

"Some friends are arriving soon," replied Derrick.

"What does Australia want with India?" pressed the man, but Derrick steered the conversation away from politics.

"We've got our best eleven turning up to play cricket, it's gonna be great."

"Cricket?" said the man, knowing Derrick had just paid him off. "Okay, I thought it might be something to do with strategic power balance and the Quad."

Derrick just shrugged and stared ahead at the dark silhouette slowly coming into dock.

"Enjoy the cricket, mate. Maybe you can make a beer snake," said the man, walking off unimpressed.

"Who was that dude?" said the Bulldog.

"Just one of the workers," replied Derrick, starting to wonder if everyone was an Australian spy.

Bulldog photographed the *Charleston* coming alongside the deep-water container port on golden hour with the connection between the military and the economy beautifully captured.

Derrick spent the night on the *Charleston* and in the morning the Task Group followed three Indian Destroyers deep into the Indian Ocean. He needed to get back to the frigate he sailed to India on, which meant transferring ships out at sea while underway.

A Boatswain monitored the ship-to-ship transfer, and he opened the side hatch that exposed the vastness of the ocean and the enormity of the warship. "When I say go, make sure you maintain three points of contact on the ladder and step down to the boat quickly," he shouted.

Palms clammy, Derrick nodded. Falling in the drink was not an option.

The frigate's powerboat came alongside and pushed into *Charleston's* side. The warship cut through the ocean like butter, but the powerboat was victim to the rise and fall of the crashing waves. Derrick felt like a tiny spec on the face of the planet — one slip and the universe would welcome him home. He made his way down the rope ladder but the powerboat fell away with the swell.

"Let go! Now!" yelled the Boatswain.

Derrick took a deep breath and let go of the ladder, and in the split second before the sailor below pulled him into the boat, he thought he'd fallen to his doom.

"Welcome aboard," yelled the sailor while Derrick lay wedged to the floor. "You've got to watch that gap. We've lost too many people because they've hung on to the rope when the boat drifts away."

"Glad I didn't know that!" Derrick yelled back.

Bulldog quickly followed and he also came down with a thud. Once they sat in position, the powerboat broke away from the ship.

Derrick had received an order from his higher headquarters to capture the two countries submarine hunting together; to send a message that the global rules-based order must be upheld and the Quad was the partnership to enforce it.

"Welcome to *HMAS Miranda,* Derrick," said the Executive Officer once they had made it to the frigate. "You've got run of the ship, but don't bother the CO. Come and see me first before you bother her."

"Can we get access to Blue Ring and its crew?" asked Derrick. "We need to show we're capable of destroying threats to our sea lanes." Blue Ring was the warship's helicopter, a lethal submarine hunter and Derrick's best shot at telling a good news story.

"The crew are asleep, but they'll be at orders at 1600 in air ops. Just knock on the door and introduce yourself, they'll be wrapped," said the XO with a laugh.

That night, Derrick looked out from the deck as the moon lit the ocean and the stars became a navigation aid. It was perfect conditions for flying and Blue Ring had a full combat load. Submarines were stalking the Task Group, and Bulldog had filmed the orders to hunt and destroy them. They'd set up cameras on the bridge and in the operations room and were listening intently to radio traffic when an Indian destroyer radioed in.

"Call sign Blue Ring on task, two enemy submarines known to be in the vicinity."

Combat systems operators monitored their screens, and a soft green glow illuminated the operations room.

"Derrick to the CO's cabin," was next to come over the PA, and the operators stared at Derrick like he was in the shit.

Fuck, here we go? Leaving Bulldog to continue recording, Derrick walked to the CO's cabin and knocked on the door. *What could she possibly want with me.*

"Come in, Derrick," called the CO.

Entering, Derrick observed that the CO was in a white uniform, which was unusual during an exercise. She pointed for him to sit in front of her desk. Another Navy Captain, also in whites, sat towards the CO and Derrick couldn't make out if he was Australian or Indian.

"Derrick, meet Captain Singh. He attended the Australian Naval College when he was an officer cadet."

Derrick shook Singh's hand and immediately realised he was the officer that almost prevented them from leaving the port when they'd first arrived.

"Nice to meet you," said Captain Singh. "I read your Sri Lankan piece in the Daily Mirror."

Derrick wasn't aware of an article making it to the news but was glad it hit the mark.

"It's true our region has many threats: terrorism, malign influence, economic coercion and now trade routes being impeded. We need to demonstrate our shared commitment to safeguarding our region from these threats." Captain Singh's voice was getting louder. "Only true friends exercise their submarine capabilities together, and that is what we are doing here. Submarine hunting — together."

Right on time the CO's radio crackled to life. "Ma'am this is the Officer of the Watch, call sign Blue Ring has located and destroyed one enemy submarine."

"Nil reports of a second submarine, call sign Blue Ring has been called off station and will re-task. Officer of the Watch out."

"Thanks for dropping by, Derrick," said the CO. "I look forward to seeing your work."

Captain Singh stood up and shook Derrick's hand. "Our countries will be working more closely in the future. I hope to see you again soon."

Derrick thanked them both and went back to the bridge to find Bulldog.

"Man, you missed the whole thing," said Bulldog. "Torpedoes were locked on us and everything."

"Mate, the Indians loved our Sri Lankan piece," replied Derrick. "We have to nail this exercise and get the package to the press."

After a week at sea capturing vision that was likely to make the news, they sent their product back to Canberra expecting for it to hit the headlines immediately. But days later, not even an acknowledgement of its receipt had been returned.

"Why aren't the war games in the news?" asked Bulldog. "We're leaving India and everyone's expecting it …"

"Must be some bloody reason for the embargo," said Derrick, not hiding his frustration. "Nice of the strategic gurus back home to keep us in the dark though, I love these conversations with COs."

Disgruntled, Derrick went to stand on the flight deck to watch India fade in the distance. He pulled out his phone to see that he still had reception, and looked in hope to see if Emily had messaged him.

It's like you're dead, read a message from Charlie. *Whose boyfriend never texts or calls when they're away???*

Derrick hadn't spoken to Charlie in weeks. He'd wanted to call to say hello, but knew he was likely to get a response that could send him over the edge, so he'd concentrated on work. He stared out at the ocean and rolled the dice.

Hey Charlie, tried to call — internet down again. I'll be in Thailand in a few days, will try you there.

CHAPTER 16

The crew looked ragged having been deployed for over a month and they were due for a few days of rest and respite in Thailand. *HMA Ships Charleston* and *Miranda* dropped their anchors in Patong Bay off the island of Phuket, just in time to watch the sun rise over dark mountains that fell into a glistening ocean.

Ferries met them at their ocean berths, and made regular trips delivering the crew ashore. Derrick had booked a hotel at the end of the party strip on Bangla Road, and as soon as he checked in he fell asleep to the echoes of seafood markets beginning for the day. When he woke, the night markets were in full swing and he stepped out to bustling crowds and the smell of smoking coconut husks.

The Task Group Chief Warrant Officer was turning fifty and he'd invited the crew to the Tiger Nightclub; where the girls twirled through neon hoops and Russian bouncers mercilessly policed the crowd. Derrick pushed his way through the throng to join Bulldog at the bar where it seemed one of the bouncers was educating him on club etiquette.

"Touch the girls and I touch you," said the bouncer after a dancer had sat on Bulldog's lap to lure him in for a kiss.

For once, Bulldog surrendered and he gently pushed the girl off his lap who continued to tease the crowd. Derrick sighed with a laugh; some things never change. He sat on a stool next to Bulldog who already had a couple of beers lined up, before an overweight street hawker brushed by him and shoved her finger under his lip.

"Fifty Baht," said the woman with a toothless smile.

"You put a dirty finger in my mouth, shove some shit under my lip and now you want fifty Baht!" cried Derrick.

"She got me too," said Bulldog and he pulled back his upper lip to show Derrick the tobacco pouch.

"Oh, that's ok then," Derrick replied before handing over the money then spitting the snuff into an ashtray.

The club went on forever inside and attractive ladyboys sat at tables enticing the tourists to sit with them.

"Drink with us," one of them beckoned, grabbing Derrick by the hand pulling him to the table.

"I'm just going through to the men's room," said Derrick in a state of confused interest.

"When you come back," she said as she/he let go of his hand.

When he returned, two more women grabbed an arm each and tried to pull him to different tables. Bulldog recorded it with his phone in one hand and with the other pushed Derrick to one of the seats.

"Where you from sexy boy?" asked the woman seated next to Derrick, batting her fake eyelashes and crossing her long slender legs.

"Australia, where are you from?"

"Bangkok," and she slid her hand high up his thigh.

With clenched butt cheeks Derrick stood bolt upright as the woman and Bulldog laughed.

"Chill mate, they're just having a laugh," said Bulldog, putting his arm around Derrick.

"I have to go, mate, replied Derrick. "Charlie's grinding me at the moment, and if she finds out I'm having fun with ladyboys I'll never hear the end of it."

"Where you go sexy boy, with your big Australian muscles?"

Derrick turned and walked away through the throng of excited punters, rolling his eyes when the ladyboy put her arm around Bulldog, who took his seat.

Ambling slowly back down Bangla Road, Derrick pulled out his phone.

I thought you were going to call, read Charlie's message.

Sydney was three hours in front, and Derrick's watch read midnight. He wondered if Charlie was awake and after three rings of the dial tone, she picked up.

"Where the fuck are you, Derrick?"

Music was booming along Bangla Road and Derrick found it hard to hear. "We got into Phuket today," he said. "It was one of the guy's birthdays, so we went out to celebrate."

"So, you'd rather be out with your mates than call your girlfriend."

"Babe it's not like that, everyone's out."

"Whatever. Why don't you call me when you're sober?" Charlie promptly hung up.

"Fuck …" Derrick cursed as he looked heavenward and closed his eyes. Dejected, he walked back to his room to get some sleep.

In the morning, he called again to appease Charlie's bad mood. "Hey Charlie, sorry about last night, I should have called earlier. How are you?"

"I've hurt my knee, this time it's a ligament."

"Shit, why didn't you tell me?" asked Derrick, disappointed he didn't know.

"Derrick, you never have reception and I never know where you are."

"You could email, you know … How did it happen?" asked Derrick.

"My horse, Marmalade, bucked me off at my parents' farm. She must've been fighting with the other horses and got a cut on her side. I didn't realise, and I kicked it while I was riding. Now we both have to rest for at least six weeks, which sucks; I wanted to enter us into a Polo competition."

"Polo?" said Derrick. "I didn't know you played, that's awesome!"

They spoke for an hour and Derrick thought they'd gotten rid of the negative energy that plagued their relationship, for the moment at least. He also felt like he should be at home supporting Charlie, but at the same time he wanted to know that she backed him with what he was doing. Lately, he was always disappointed about the latter and had been starting to think they'd probably be better of just being friends. But he still wanted Charlie to know he cared so he sent some flowers and promised to call in a week from Vietnam.

When they pulled up the anchor after three days, not a single person had been lost to the debauched Thai nights — an achievement most COs would be proud of. The Task Group sailed south through the Malacca straights and then north through the South China Sea.

Derrick hadn't been to Vietnam before, and all hands lined the deck when they sailed into Nha Trang, where a Vietnamese band played for their arrival. The ship's office had given him a two-day leave pass and as soon as the gangway was down, Derrick jumped on a bus to the beach. Like a foreboding warning, a thunderstorm hit just as the bus doors opened and he ran to a French cafe to call Charlie.

"I made it to Vietnam, how's Marmalade and your knee?"

"I'm better but Marmalade has an infection," said Charlie. "The vet's given her antibiotics and I bought her some colourful bandages."

"She needs bandages?" asked Derrick.

"They're to make her look pretty in polo competitions, not for her cut. Why are you in Vietnam anyway?"

"We're just being good neighbours … What's the sudden interest in polo?" asked Derrick feeling a curious sense of paranoia returning.

"My friend Sarah started playing — you can come and play when you're back."

"Sounds amazing but I'm not sure you'll want me on your side, I've never ridden before and I'm sure I'll be hopeless."

"You'll be fine, I'll teach you," said Charlie seeming to stop the conversation from moving forward. "Hey … Sarah's coming over for drinks with some friends soon, so I have to go and get ready, but call me tomorrow if you're still there." She hung up before Derrick could say goodbye and he instantly felt like shit.

Who the fuck is Sarah and friends… And what happened to tennis?

He wasn't surprised Charlie had met new people, but he also knew he wasn't getting the full story. The relationship gain he thought he'd made over the phone in Thailand seemed to have disappeared and hopelessness crept in once more.

Fuck it… I can't think like this anymore. I can't change what's happening at home, I can only be part of what's happening here.

Derrick turned off his phone, put it in his backpack, and walked to the beach for a distraction from his thoughts. He sat down at a beach bar to grab a beer and watched aggressive Russians play soccer like it was boxing.

113

Engrossed in his thoughts, he didn't notice Bulldog arrive at the bar.

"Not answering your phone, mate?" said Bulldog as he sat down. "I thought you'd be chatting to Charlie not drinking tins at the bar?"

"Charlie's getting drunk with some new friends that play polo. So, I'm having a beer in the Moscow of Vietnam … They have more styles of potato on the menu than beers."

"Ha, I see … Let's have a beer then," said Bulldog, accompanied by his usual laugh and bristling red hair.

After dark, they left the beach and wandered down the dimly lit back streets where buckets of fish spilled onto the pavement and the smell of culinary delights permeated the air. Just as Derrick began to feel like he was getting the authentic Vietnam experience they walked into a smoke-filled whiskey bar that wouldn't have been out of place on Bourbon Street in New Orleans.

"This place is an absolute mystery," said Derrick.

"Let's have a couple here, then go to Skydeck," said Bulldog. "Trip Advisor says the place pumps."

"Okay, but I better book a hotel. I won't make it back to the ship by midnight."

The Task Group Commander had imposed Cinderella leave that ordered all personnel to be in hotels or on board their ship by midnight, to avoid a late-night Vietnamese curfew.

When Derrick looked online to book, he saw the rest of the Task Group had taken all the recommended hotels. *Fuck it, I'll just book something cheap …*

They finished off a couple of American Bourbons, Derrick checked in to a hotel just down the road, then he and Bulldog caught a cab to Skydeck, where the line to get in extended far beyond the elevator to its entrance.

"Jägermeister and a beer?" asked Bulldog once they'd arrived at the bar.

"Yeah man — we don't have to work until Singapore, let's go nuts," said Derrick having lost all inhibitions.

The music pumped and they danced terribly, much to the delight of the Chinese tourists who all wanted photos with the Australian party guys. No one understood each other but smiles and crazy dance moves seemed a common language.

"This is the best night ever!" said Derrick as he high-fived Bulldog and howled like a wolf with his beer held high in the air. Catching his breath, he looked around the club. In his peripheral view he thought he saw someone staring at him from the bar. A woman in sunglasses turned and slipped back through the crowd. Derrick raced to the bar thinking he knew who it was.

"Emily," he shouted.

A group of tourists folded around the woman, and they looked at him blankly. Derrick scanned the club but saw nothing that resembled the woman's appearance.

I must be seeing things, Derrick thought. *I'm drunk and should go back to the hotel; it's got to be close to midnight.* Without saying goodbye to Bulldog, he left the bar and paced the streets looking for his hotel. He walked along the beachfront looking for an indicator but saw nothing familiar, and when he tried looking at his phone for directions, his world began to swirl. He sat against a coconut palm, closed his eyes, and pictured Emily. "I wish you were here," he said, and drifted off to sleep.

The streets were now empty and two heavily armed Vietnamese Police Officers patrolled the beach while reinforcements waited in their truck. They approached Derrick and kicked his foot to see if he would stir.

"Wake up," one of the officers said loudly. When Derrick didn't move, the officer reached inside his back pocket, pulled out his wallet and deduced from the tourist card inside that Derrick was Australian military. The two officers left Derrick where he was and one of them made a call.

"Ms Emily, one of your people is asleep on the beach," said the officer.

"Thank you, I'll come and collect him," replied Emily on the other end of the line.

A black van parked close to the Vietnamese Police truck and a smartly dressed woman got out and spoke to the two Officers on patrol.

"Thank you for speaking to me first," said Emily. "I'll make sure he gets to his hotel and then to his ship." She then handed a thick envelope to one of the Officers before two men dressed in dark clothing got out of the SUV and stood by her side. She looked through the wallet the Police Officers handed her and smiled.

"So, Derrick, it looks as if you can't handle your drink," she said. "Put him in the back of the vehicle and make sure he doesn't wake up."

The phone next to Derrick's hotel bed shrilled in his ears for what felt like forever ... Groping around until he felt the handset, he pulled it to his ear. "What?"

"Derrick, pack your things and get your arse to reception," said the Watch Commander. Derrick got his stuff together and raced to the lift. In the foyer, the Watch Commander was pacing in annoyed, jerky steps.

"The ship's been looking for you all night, you've been AWOL. Command hasn't approved this hotel for you to stay in, and you didn't tell the watch of your whereabouts. No one knew where you were!" said the Watch Commander angrily, hands on his hips.

"How did you find me then?" asked Derrick.

116

"Someone called the ship, not leaving any details. No doubt one of your fine mates. Get back to the ship, your leave has been revoked."

When Derrick got back to the ship the Coxswain slapped him with an infringement notice.

"You're lucky I'm not charging you. What have you got to say?"

"I should have put my hotel in the spreadsheet and called the watch."

"Don't be smart, Derrick, you broke the system and now the boss is removing your shore leave. You're not getting off the ship until Jakarta."

Derrick texted Bulldog to see if it was him that called the ship: *Where did you go last night?*

Ha-ha mate, you just took off. I looked for you, but you're the master of dropping smoke, so I left.

Did you call the ship?

No mate, do I need to?

*No, it's all good. I'll see you in a couple of day*s.

Derrick didn't know how he got to his room, but he thought the punishment he received didn't fit the crime. He walked up onto the deck of ship and called Charlie to see how her night was. "Hey Charlie, you'll never guess what … The CO's taken my leave off me because I forgot to put my hotel in a bloody spreadsheet! They had a search party looking for me, for God's sake."

"So let me get this straight," said Charlie. "I'm going out with one of those dickhead soldiers who goes missing overseas. Am I going to read about you in the news Derrick? Am I? What am I going to say to my friends?"

Hanging up, Derrick looked heavenward again.

God, why is it the only support I get is from the same people that just took my leave?

CHAPTER 17

The Task Group arrived in Darwin to little fanfare after three months at sea, and Derrick flew straight home to Canberra. He hadn't spoken to Charlie since his time 'absent without official leave' and was planning to go and visit her.

"Hey Charlie, I just got home … how's it going?"

"Derrick, I know you've been away for a while, but I think we need time to see other people. Our lives are going in two totally different directions and it's not fair on either of us. I'll call you in a few weeks … we need some space and time," said Charlie.

"Has anything happened at home?" asked Derrick, but Charlie had already hung up.

Fuck … What did I expect? … Do not get back into that relationship, he told himself, firm in his resolve. Although he wasn't entirely surprised, he wanted answers he knew he wouldn't get. So, he did what he always did to prevent the onset of depression — focus on work. Another trip was just around the corner if he played his cards right, and he began to study operations in the Middle East.

In Iraq, security forces had all but defeated the Islamic State, and in Afghanistan, the Afghan National Army now had the lead for defeating the Taliban. The Australian Government had lost interest in protracted campaigns and was becoming increasingly interested on issues closer to home. Derrick began to wonder whether a trip was on the cards, after all.

"Team, trips to the Middle East are wrapping up," said Derrick's CO at the weekly round table. "The Chief of the Defence Force is focused on our region and therefore so are we. Having said that, the graduate will be going to Iraq. He's just come out of the college and needs the experience. Derrick, you might get lucky on the rotation after that — if there is one."

Derrick walked out of the meeting and grabbed Bulldog for a chat. "Replaced again," said Derrick, standing outside. "By a fucking graduate. I bet this is because of the AWOL thing in Vietnam."

"Don't worry, mate, something'll come up," said Bulldog. "They always do."

The National Security Committee sat mid-year, and it agreed on another rotation to Iraq and Afghanistan, but with drastically reduced manning. The halls of power in Canberra were deciding again what was best for military operations, and sealing many a soldier's fate.

Derrick's team was in a period of down time, and he and Bulldog were on courses in Queensland when the CO called.

"Derrick, NSC just sat and Iraq is still on. Headquarters hasn't released numbers yet, so plan as if you're going. Let Bulldog know too, you're both going to Darwin."

They arrived in Darwin in the middle of the 'build up' where the heat builds through the day, but the storm clouds don't break. It was hot, and by the time Derrick got his bags to the accommodation, he was wet with sweat.

"Wet t-shirt competitions died in the nineties, mate," said Bulldog when he saw Derrick's nipples.

"Shut up Bulldog, give me a hand," said Derrick and they threw his bags in his room.

The public had lost interest in the reporting from Iraq and Afghanistan, which suited the Government, who said little about it. Derrick saw the writing on the wall and told Bulldog it was unlikely they would be going. "Mate, no one cares about operations in the Middle East anymore. All Canberra cares about is the Indo-Pacific."

"You don't think we're going, do you?" said Bulldog.

"I'm just saying be prepared to go home."

"You only know for sure when you're on the plane. Until then, we might as well be on holiday," said Bulldog, laughing as he cracked open a beer and turned up the music on his balcony.

Derrick understood that Bulldog, also recently single again, was hitting the town hard. He'd been swiping left and right on dating apps since his arrival and had been on some disastrous dates in pursuit of love.

"Hey, can I borrow the car this weekend?" said Bulldog.

"Yeah why?" asked Derrick, knowing full well Bulldog was up to something.

"I've been chatting to this girl and she's flying up from Adelaide."

"From Adelaide?"

"Yeah, I'll take her to the national park like we're backpackers. It'll be fun." Bulldog gave him a smug look.

"Can't you get any birds round here?" said Derrick. "Fucking Adelaide."

"Righto, Grandad," said Bulldog. "I'll call you afterwards, to come meet us for a drink. It'll stop you moping around base all weekend."

Jealous of Bulldog's ability to continually pursue women despite being frequently rejected, Derrick asked, "How can you be bothered to chase girls all the time?"

"Jesus, Derrick, just have some fun, man. Life's not all serious."

Never-ending fights with Charlie had destroyed Derrick's confidence, and he'd all but lost his enthusiasm to engage with the opposite sex. He agreed to meet Bulldog when he got back from his dating adventure, but it was late when he called and Derrick was fast asleep.

"Mate, come into town. This bird's gone berserk!" Bulldog laughed nervously.

"Beserk how? What happened?" asked Derrick.

"We had a pretty good day, well it wasn't weird or anything," said Bulldog. "We had a few drinks at the hotel, but in the first bar we go into she starts dancing by herself on the dance floor, and this weird couple came up to her and kissed her. She was shaking her ass and grinding all over these people. I thought cool this is my escape and walked out, then she chased after me. I took her back to the hotel and said goodnight and she started screaming. She said that she came here for me, and I needed to take her out."

"Where are you now?" asked Derrick.

"In a hotel at the other end of town," Bulldog replied.

"All right, I'll come and meet you." Derrick caught a cab and met Bulldog in the city where the clubs were heaving.

"Look, she's over there," said Bulldog, pointing. Derrick looked over and saw a Barbie doll blonde take the hand of a bikie and walk him out of a club on the Darwin strip.

"Fuck, Bulldog, I'm surprised she didn't feed you to the crocodiles."

The next morning Derrick woke up with Bulldog's arms wrapped around him in a loving embrace, and his phone once again ringing hot.

"Hello," said Derrick hoarsely.

"Derrick, the boss wants to speak to you," said a Major on the other end of the line. "He'll be back at 15:00. Make sure you're at Headquarters when he gets there."

The Major hung up and Derrick instantly felt sick. "Fuck, we're being removed."

"From the trip?" asked Bulldog with his arms still around Derrick.

"No, from the hotel — yes, from the trip, we're fucking off the trip, I know it. And get off me ..."

Derrick and Bulldog packed their things and arrived at headquarters.

"I'll get to the point," said the Lieutenant Colonel. "Cabinet reduced the numbers of personnel for this trip and Ops has decided on the positions. Unfortunately, they cut yours. Boys I'm sorry, but you're off the trip."

Sombre and dehydrated, Derrick and Bulldog left headquarters.

"Ah, it's all good," said Bulldog outside in the searing heat. "Something'll come up. I might see if there's a flight for Canberra tonight."

Derrick hugged Bulldog, who then made his way to the airport. *I wonder if he'll see Barbie there?*

At dinner, Derrick sat down with the Major and told him Bulldog had just flown home. "I'll fly home tomorrow," he added. He said goodbye to his friends and went to sleep keen to get on with his life.

The next morning, he ate breakfast alone until the Major walked into the mess and sat in front of him.

"Don't get too comfortable in Canberra, Derrick. We want you back in a week, without Bulldog," said the Major. "Somebody is trying desperately to get you on this trip."

Derrick was confused, but he flew from Darwin happy there was still a chance of deploying and when he got home, he collapsed in bed. After a couple of days at home, no one had called or messaged, so he booked a flight to Darwin that left at the end of the week.

Time enough for a beer at the Old Lyneham Inn, he thought, and walked through the chill of a Canberra night to the dimly lit bar.

Couples sat conversing, cosy next to the fire and a folk guitarist had hypnotised a small crowd. Derrick sat in an old-fashioned booth and stared at the music man through the end of his beer glass. He went to the bar to get another beer but when he returned a woman had taken his seat and was rummaging through her handbag. Derrick turned away. "Sorry, I'll find another table."

"Derrick," called a soft voice. The woman's deep blue eyes and long blonde hair took him aback.

"Wow … Emily, you look amazing," said Derrick.

"You look a bit different out of uniform yourself," said Emily. "And what's an Army Officer doing alone in an old bikie bar?"

"It's a bit of a story. Can I get you a drink?" asked Derrick.

Emily smiled. "I'll have one G&T, thank you."

They spoke for hours, and the drinks kept coming. She told Derrick of the sadness of losing a friend in the Sri Lankan bombings, and her fondness of the people there.

"What happened to the soldiers you were with?" asked Derrick.

"They completed their training and went home," Emily said rather abruptly. "I'm getting posted again soon. Another country, another set of problems."

"Where are you off to?" enquired Derrick.

"The Embassy in Baghdad," said Emily, and she gazed into Derrick's eyes for a moment longer than usual. "To represent Australia's interests." She laughed and draped her arms around Derrick.

"We she should probably get you home," said Derrick when Emily hung on to him and kissed him.

"Okay, we probably should," she murmured, with a coy laugh. "We don't want an incident like in Vietnam…"

"Vietnam???"

Derrick dropped Emily home in a cab, and watched her fumble for the keys to her house. He looked at the time on his phone and saw that Charlie had left a message. *Every fucking time,* thought Derrick.

Call me … read Charlie's message.

Derrick arrived in Darwin a day later than planned. No one was the wiser when he strolled into headquarters asking for the Major.

"Derrick!" yelled the Major after hearing his voice. "How was your leave?"

"I'm not sure. I spoke to Charlie my ex-girlfriend on the very last day and I think we got back together," said Derrick nervously.

"Well, I'm sure six months in the Middle East will reinforce your love for each other. It's good to have you back all the same, your old mate Russian has turned up too. The Commanding Officer of the mentoring team will have a chat to you both shortly, but I want you to know it was the Commander that pulled this one off. He got you two on the trip."

124

CHAPTER 18

It was a winter morning in Iraq and Emily stood shivering in the rain at the Baghdad Diplomatic Support Centre, across the runway from the international airport. Most rocket strikes occurred at night, and Iran's proxies were hitting their targets with increasing accuracy. The Militia groups frequently targeted the airport with indirect fire and the runway was lined with pockmarked concrete T-Walls.

Emily watched a RAAF Hercules land and a company of armed soldiers walk into customs. She called her security detail and got back into a blacked-out SUV that was parked alongside the runway. "They're here."

"Acknowledged Ma'am," said the man on the other end of the line.

Derrick's rifle was slung over his shoulder and his left hand held the foregrip close to his body. With his right hand he presented his passport to the Iraqi official, who looked at him with deep resentment.

"Assalamu alaikum," said Derrick. His greeting was met with silence.

"Look in the camera," said the Iraqi.

Derrick looked ahead while the man took his photo, then gave his passport back with a blank stare.

"Shukran," said Derrick, and he went to sit down in the waiting area.

The weather was miserable and so were their hosts — it seemed everyone wanted the Coalition out of Iraq. They were on a training mission, not combat operations, but after decades of war and terrorism the Iraqis didn't see a military uniform as a sign of peace.

The soldiers were due to fly into Camp Cooke Airbase at midday, but a storm cell sat above it and the Herc couldn't get in to land. The camp had recently been hit with 107mm Katyusha rockets as a warning for the

Coalition to leave Iraq, and Derrick could feel nervous energy in the air.

"Derrick, with Bulldog gone you're our imagery capability," said the Commander. "I need you to document the battle damage, I want the evidence in case we end up in a Royal Commission."

"Yes, Sir."

Derrick took hold of his camera and pointed it at the Russian.

"Are you in love with me?" asked the Russian.

"What?" replied Derrick.

"Don't point that thing at me."

"It's for your own good, your mum will want your photo when you're dead," said Derrick.

"Fuck you, Derrick," said the Russian pointing at his face.

"Russian, come with me," said the Commander, standing and walking away with the intelligence staff through the gate to the diplomatic centre. They didn't return.

Great. Where are they going? thought Derrick.

A U.S. contractor called the remaining members by name to get back on their flight. Derrick was called last, and as he left the waiting room a burly bloke pulled him to the side and told him to wait. The contractor marched the other members to the aircraft then gave the thumbs up to the aircrew and Derrick heard the engines spool.

"What the fuck's going on?" shouted Derrick at his handler.

"Calm down princess, you'll scare the locals," said an Australian voice. "We're getting a helo to the Green Zone, no one will miss ya."

The handler walked out onto the flight line and Derrick followed.

"Fuck … I've just got here," yelled Derrick, but the rotor wash drowned out his voice. Two US Black Hawks waited on the tarmac and their rotors turned the rain into mist. As they approached the aircraft the aircrew waved them both onboard and connected their headsets.

"Dagger one three, cleared for take-off," said the air traffic control tower.

"Copy Baghdad tower, Dagger one three cleared for take-off. We're oscar mike," said the pilot.

Before Derrick knew he'd left the ground, the sprawl of Baghdad was in sight. They flew hidden in the clouds to Union III and flared aggressively on their decent. *This is the kind of shit I've been waiting for,* thought Derrick, struggling to control his excitement.

He followed his handler from the helicopter to an up-armoured black SUV that was waiting in the rain. The handler opened the back door and Derrick got in.

"Welcome to Baghdad," said a voice with a strong Australian accent from the front passenger seat. "Emily told me of your arrival," he said just as the door next to Derrick opened.

"Thanks for dropping by," said Emily, getting in next to him. "It's just a short drive to the Embassy."

Derrick's handler got in the front seat and began to drive while a second SUV pulled in behind them.

"The Embassy, why am I not surprised?" said Derrick, "Nice to see you, Emily."

"Derrick, this is Mr Thomas Kent. He's in Baghdad with a trade envoy," said Emily.

"Pleased to meet you, mate," said Mr Kent.

The SUV parked outside the Australian Embassy and the handler motioned to Derrick to wait while Iraqi security looked underneath the SUV for improvised explosive devices and bomb detection dogs sniffed the outside of the vehicle. A security detail then cleared their entry, and the handler gave the all-clear to move inside.

"Give me your rifle," said the handler. "Don't worry mate, you'll get it back."

Derrick followed Emily and Mr Kent through the Embassy to the executive suites. Emily opened the door and when they went through Derrick saw that canapés had been prepared and sparkling wine sat on trays.

"Can I offer you a drink?" asked Mr Kent.

"No, Sir, but the canapes look good," said Derrick as he helped himself.

"Mr Kent is here on behalf of Australian grain producers at the request of the Australian Government," said Emily. "Grain is worth over $200 million to the Australian economy and both the Iraqis and our people depend on it."

"It works like this," said Mr Kent. "America needs Iraq's oil and the Iraqis need American dolleriedoos. But if Iraqi Government policy doesn't suit the Americans, like when a Shia-aligned President sides with Iranian interests, the US won't let them withdraw from US Banks ... The Americans control their economy."

Derrick nabbed another canape and nodded to show that he was following the logic.

"We don't have that luxury ... but we benefit from the status quo so we can get paid for our grain. The Iraqis need our grain just like they need their money from the Americans. We help the Iraqis and they help us ... so we need an Iraqi Government that can facilitate both our interests."

Mr Kent turned around to pick up a second glass of wine while Derrick automatically mirrored his action. Emily who noticed the faux pas, casually moved next to him, and removed it before Derrick knew what had happened and before Mr Kent went on ...

"Now, the Islamic State were cowboys, thrust on the world through social media, and the security forces can handle them. But the Militia groups … Iran controls them, and they don't want us here."

"Remember when we were in Sri Lanka?" said Emily. "We changed public perceptions because of our shared interest — to protect Sri Lankans. It's the same here, but with far greater risk. We're here at the request of the Iraqi Government. If the Militia get their way and remove Coalition support to Iraq, our influence and trade go with it."

"So, what next Ma'am?" Derrick asked.

"When you arrive at Camp Cooke, Akil will meet you — he's an Iraqi soon to be an American interpreter — but he works for me," said Emily. "He'll take you to your accommodation while the rest of your group are in briefs. Akil has explained where you are to be."

"Where am I to be?" asked Derrick.

"Taking photos. No-one will ask questions because you carry the camera. Akil will provide you with imagery of the people we're interested in.

"Shia Militia?" asked Derrick but Emily continued without acknowledging the question.

"I'd like you to photograph these people when they are in your company. Keep a photographic essay and store it on this thumb drive." Emily handed him a silver thumb drive. "This is an encrypted drive and only you and I will have the key. Woody will come and collect it when we need it," said Emily, pointing at Derrick's handler standing at the door. "And Derrick … No-one knows of this meeting, so please think twice about mentioning it to anyone."

"See ya later, mate," said Mr Kent and he shook Derrick's hand.

"I'll be in touch," said Emily, and she kissed him on the cheek.

Woody took his cue and opened the door, so Derrick nodded goodbye and left the suite.

"I'll take you to Camp Cooke," said Woody, walking toward the SUV. "We'll meet Akil, and he can give you a ground brief." At the SUV, he handed Derrick back his rifle. "See, would I lie to you, mate?" Woody winked.

The Black Hawks were still turning and burning on the tarmac when Derrick and Woody arrived at the flightline. The aircrew were already in their seats, and waved them straight onboard. Gunners scanned the ground for targets as they left Forward Operating Base Union III.

After a half-hour flight, they arrived at Camp Cooke where a dilapidated sign welcomed them to the Airbase. *Welcome to Camp Cooke Airbase – home of the Tigris pineapple.*

Akil was waiting at the Terminal when they landed and Woody gave a low-key hand gesture to say hello.

"Assalamu alaikum," said Akil, leaning back on the bonnet of his SUV.

"Fuck, it looks like we missed the war," said Derrick. "This place is deserted."

The camp looked like a Forward Operating Base ... but depleted of troops. AH-64 Apache gunships sat overhead, and helicopters lined the tarmac, but things seemed slow.

"This is the end of the mission, mate, security's restored," said Woody. "We're done training these guys. It'll be counter terrorism ops and that's it."

They drove from the terminal and Derrick wondered what it was like during Operation Iraqi Freedom, or when the Islamic State were still in Mosul.

They parked at the base coffee shop and Akil handed Derrick a brown envelope. "Put this in your pocket," said Akil. "Your room key is in there with photos and instructions. Your bed has been made and you have a roommate, the Russian. Go get a coffee, your friend is waiting."

"What about the ground brief?" asked Derrick.

"There's plenty of time," said Akil. "Go and see your friend."

Derrick got out of the car into the mud and sloshed over to the coffee shop.

"Derrick!" yelled the Russian. "The coffee is shit."

CHAPTER 19

It was pitch black and raining just before dawn the next morning when an IED detonated on route Tampa that ran alongside Camp Cooke. Derrick had spent the night in bed staring at the roof of his accommodation pod waiting for an attack and the explosion sent him to the floor.

"Incoming, get your fucking armour on!" Derrick yelled at the Russian who was still sound asleep.

"Go back to sleep, baby," said the Russian, rolling back over.

Derrick waited on the floor for a few minutes, until he heard a muffled conversation outside his room. He leaped up, and on opening his door saw an Australian Corporal standing in the dark talking to the Operations Centre.

The Corporal dropped his radio and looked at him. "The Iraqis found an Islamic State IED dug into the road. They just didn't tell anyone they were going to blow it."

Now wide awake, Derrick decided he might as well go and check out what was happening outside. Low-lying storm clouds framed the T-walls and muddy accommodation lanes, while a lonely figure holding an umbrella hobbled through the dark. As she passed Derrick down the lane she stopped.

"Are we being hit?" asked an Iraqi woman with emerald eyes.

"It was a controlled detonation by the Army," said Derrick who had begun to shiver in the cold.

"Ah okay," said the woman as she calmly smiled and hobbled off to work.

IED Blasts and Rocket attacks are the new normal ... Get used to it, Derrick told himself.

An alert tone sounded across the base and the PA system crackled to life. "All clear — all clear — all clear," rang out as the sunrise slowly illuminated a misty camp.

After a shower and a shave Derrick walked back to his pod and put his uniform on for the day. He pulled over his head his chest rig with ballistic plates, strapped a pistol to his hip and put on his helmet. Before going outside, he grabbed his rifle and quickly checked safe. The Russian was good at playing tricks and Derrick wouldn't put it past his friend to 'accidently' put his weapon on instant.

A wet and muddy path led to the dining facility and Derrick started to get his bearings as he walked to get breakfast. Most of the camp were still asleep when he ordered from the omelette bar and sat down alone.

Akil walked in shortly after and poured himself a coffee. "Derrick, good morning ... how did you sleep?" Akil sat down next to him.

"It seems I don't need an alarm clock," said Derrick.

"The Militia planted the IED, not Islamic State — they are mostly dead. They plant the IEDs, then tip off the Army and the Islamic State gets the blame ... It's a game."

"Why do they do that?" replied Derrick.

"Credibility ... To demonstrate the Militia and Army have intel and they'll share it when they want to. It's also a win for the Militia if they hit a food truck supplying the Coalition."

"Aren't we supporting Iraq here?"

"Yes, but Iran wants control of Iraq, and the Coalition is in the way. Iraqis protest against Iranian influence but the Militia kill them in the street. A civil war is brewing, and the Coalition needs to remain."

Derrick felt an incredible weight mounting on his shoulders and was beginning to see that the U.S. – Iranian competition for influence in the region was multi-generational. *I wonder if Geoff and Kate know I'm in an extension of their conflict.*

"Are the men in the images I gave you the Militia?" questioned Derrick when Akil paused in thought.

"Yes, they helped the Iraq Army clear Islamic State from Iraq."

"What do you need from me?" asked Derrick.

"You'll see them when we work with the Iraqi troops. I'll introduce you as the media guy and they'll get used to you documenting the trip. Just go about your business as usual, but capture any change in dynamic."

The Army guarantees our security from the Militias, and we're losing our influence thought Derrick as he finished his omelette and walked outside with Akil.

Akil drove Derrick out the gates of Camp Cooke's Green Zone to the Iraq Army's 9th Brigade Headquarters. When they arrived, the mood in the operations room was tense. Militia attacks on civilians in Baghdad had led to the resignation of the Iraqi Prime Minister, and the U.S. had recently attacked their headquarters in response to strikes on Coalition Bases. The situation was fraught.

They met with the 9th Brigade Commander, Brigadier General Khalil, and Akil introduced Derrick as a media officer.

"Derrick will help broadcast Iraq's success against The Islamic State to the world," said Akil.

Wondering how the fuck he was going to achieve that, Derrick smiled politely and snapped away with his camera.

A few weeks went by, and Derrick had indeed become a familiar fixture. He'd heard the Brigade Commander's stories repetitiously and regularly attended their ceremonies.

134

"Two thousand soldiers returned to the Iraq Army today, mate, you should've gotten out of your hole and come to the parade," said Derrick to the Russian when he returned from work one day.

"Returned from where, baby?" the Russian replied, still lying on his bed.

"They fled when the Islamic State took over Mosul."

"So, they fell for a marketing campaign and now they're back, big deal. It's New Year's Eve, baby, and I'm watching the U.S. Embassy get overrun by the Militia."

"You what?"

"Marines have flown in to secure it, and Apaches from base are on station. New Year Eve — Iraqi style," said the Russian, who burst out laughing.

News quickly spread of a rapid reaction force mobilising out of the U.S. and all of a sudden Derrick knew the war was back on. The Coalition Commander prepared the base to house incoming personnel and over the course of a couple of days Black Hawks began delivering non-essential personnel from the Baghdad Green Zone.

"Derrick, wake up," said the Russian on a grey and miserable morning. "The U.S. whacked Soleimani overnight."

"Who's Soleimani?" said Derrick.

"The Iranian Quds Force General. Fuck … and they killed a Militia Commander," the Russian said with unusual panic in his voice. "It was tit-for-tat U.S. versus Militia strikes, but the General … this is war."

"I guess both the Militia and Iran are going to want revenge now," said Derrick while staring at his roof waiting for rockets to drop.

"The Iraqi Parliament is holding an emergency meeting to remove U.S. Forces from Iraq," the Russian continued after receiving a text from the operations room.

The Coalition Commander increased security measures and limited personnel movements — no-one was to leave their accommodation pods after dark.

Media agencies around the world reported a three-day period of Iranian national mourning and Derrick suspected the worst was yet to come. After five days of little to no information through the media or otherwise, Derrick joined a night patrol at the flight line with a U.S. combat camera operator — nick-named Killer.

"Mate, helicopters should be landing shortly, and a C-17 won't be far behind," said the Patrol Commander over the radio in the Bushmaster Protected Mobility Vehicle. "We'll stay here until the Militia put up a drone to surveil us. We'll have to go take it down once it's airborne, so you're on your own then, if you want to stay here."

Black Hawks and Spanish Pumas continued to fly evacuees from the Green Zone, and Apaches on overwatch flew dark without lights. Evacuees ran across the tarmac to the safety of an American compound adjacent to the flight line and Derrick and Killer captured imagery of the panic.

"Y'all want to shoot with night vision," said Killer with a southern drawl and a long attachment fixed to her camera.

Derrick looked through the view finder and instantly knew media agencies would froth for the images. They shot the evacuation, then the Patrol Commander got orders to move.

"All right folks, we're moving out. It doesn't look like the C-17s are coming so you can stay here, or we can drop you back at the accommodation."

Derrick and the U.S. photographer looked at each other in silent agreement. "We'll take the ride back," said Derrick.

It was after midnight by the time Derrick got back. He sparked a cigarette and cracked a non-alcoholic beer; it was the closest thing to feeling drunk.

Fuck, what a night … With his head swirling with images, Derrick took off his body armour and lay on the bed ready to pass out. He succumbed to the hum of the air conditioner and fell into a deep sleep.

Minutes later Akil thumped on his door. "Derrick! Russian! Get up!"

Derrick was passed-out and the Russian answered the door. "What, Akil?"

"Iran has launched ballistic missiles aimed at Erbil, Camp Cooke and Ain Al-Assad."

"I don't care, go back to sleep," said the Russian.

"Derrick, get the fuck up!" yelled Akil.

The sound of the base alarm jolted Derrick to life. He struggled putting on his helmet and body armour, grabbed his rifle and then ran to the bunker where he dropped to his knees in the dirt. His heartbeat pounded through his eardrums, and he slowed his breathing to regain composure. *Incoming — incoming — incoming* rang out across the public address system.

"Five theatre ballistic missiles — two minutes till impact," yelled an Infantry Captain relaying information from the Operations Centre. "They've just seen eleven missiles slam into Ain Al-Assad."

Two long minutes went by … Deep thuds in the distance echoed across the landscape and a low rumble and mild shudder made dust caught in the torchlight sprinkle like snow. Derrick stared at the silhouettes lining the bunker and drifted in and out of consciousness. A base-wide roll-call confirmed no casualties or injuries five hours later and 'all clear' rang out across base.

What happened to the missiles aimed at us? thought Derrick as he opened the door to his room.

"Shut the fucken door!" yelled the Russian who hadn't left his bed. "It's five in the morning."

Derrick paused, then tracked backwards closing the door. He decided to call his higher formation, but when he did the line rang out …

Where the fuck are they? Iranian Missiles lit up Iraq last night. How could his chain of command be unavailable? Had something happened that he didn't know about? He paced in agitation and kept trying to contact his headquarters, until Akil and Killer spotted him and rushed over.

"Yo, my pictures are front page news right now," said Killer.

Derrick looked at the New York Times, CNN, BBC then the ABC. Media agencies had syndicated Killer's imagery across the globe, except in Australia it seemed. 'Night of Devastation,' read one tabloid.

After another hour Derrick still hadn't had a reply from anyone. Frantic, he walked to his office with a lit cigarette hanging out his mouth, smoking it with both hands holding his rifle. Akil and Killer walked with him to calm his frustration.

"Your country is fighting forest fires," said Akil. "I don't think anyone in Sydney or Melbourne cares about what happens here."

"Yeah, seems so," said Derrick.

"No one cares about Iraq, the bombs, the families, the …" Akil stopped. "Don't worry about selling your story back home. We need you here Derrick; we're fighting a war against Iran and your images are like bullets. The quicker you see that, the less you will care about headlines back home." Pausing, Akil looked at his buzzing phone. "We leave in fifteen minutes. The Brigade Commander wants to meet with the Coalition staff."

Brigadier Khalil knew the Coalition forces had been up all night, and it was the first time the Iraqis had met with them since the U.S. had killed Soleimani. Three up-armoured Toyota Land Cruisers moved the Coalition Commander and his staff from the base Green Zone through the fortified gates to the Iraqi headquarters. Akil followed behind the convoy in a light-skinned Mitsubishi Pajero, while Derrick looked through his camera in shotgun.

When they arrived, an Iraqi Colonel welcomed them. "Come," he said, ushering them through the operations room floor to Brigadier Khalil's office. They waited in silence for an hour before the Commander yelled through the door, summoning them into his opulent surrounds.

"We are in a difficult position," said Brigadier Khalil, reclining in his chair. "You're under our care on this base, and we're friends with the Coalition. But the Americans have killed one of our leaders and they are no longer welcome."

A man in military uniform, who Derrick recognised from Akil's pictures, walked into the office and sat next to Brigadier Khalil. Akil didn't acknowledge the man's entrance and spoke before anyone else had built up the nerve.

"The Coalition is not here as part of a proxy war," said Akil. "The Iraq Government invited them to train your soldiers, which they have. The program hasn't changed, and they will assist your soldiers until the government says not to."

The Brigadier smiled at the man seated next to him, then yelled to his butler waiting on his beck and call, "Get our guests some tea!"

Derrick picked up his camera and snapped away, knowing that something had just changed. *Have we begun training the enemy?*

CHAPTER 20

The 82nd Airborne Division had mobilised out of Fort Bragg, North Carolina, and as night fell the first of several U.S. C-17s landed. Over the coming days Camp Cooke received an extra battle group of combat power and if the base wasn't a target before, it certainly became one. Despite promises of protection from Brigadier Khalil, it didn't take a huge leap of imagination to see the Shia Militia move from Baghdad and surround Camp Cooke.

The sun was setting over Camp Cooke's 600 metre range when Derrick knelt in the dirt to adjust a young Iraqi's M16. The call to prayer began over the loud speakers and Akil told the soldiers to unload and return to their units.

"Things seem quiet," said Derrick.

"Iran might have retaliated — but the Militia hasn't. The strike that killed Soleimani also killed their leader Muhandis. They'll strike back when politically convenient," replied Akil.

Derrick motioned to a man watching them as the sun dipped lower and lower, and took his picture knowing full well the man would be silhouetted by the sun. *Clever, he knows we can't see who he is from this distance …*

"Militia," said Akil. "He's watching us training his troops."

Dusk was always hauntingly calm. Stray dogs howled and burning rubbish turned the sun dark orange as it sunk below T-walls and bunkers. Most days, Derrick lit a cigarette inside his bunker and would stare out to the runway and begin to meditate. He'd watch his thoughts float in and out of his mind and eventually come back to life when a C-17 landed, or the Apaches flew on a mission. *This place is out of control,* he thought, loving his new reality.

The Apache air weapons team had just taken off when Derrick felt a presence behind him and heard a cigarette being lit. "Akil, why do you always creep up on me?"

"Akil's gone, mate," said a familiar voice.

Derrick spun around. "Fucking hell, Woody! Where'd you come from?"

"Listen mate, I need a bit of a favour." Woody looked grim. "The soldiers you've been training on the range, a couple of them are known Militia. The old bloke watches to make sure his recruits feel the Militia's presence. They're not keen on an insider attack because they know you guys can sort them out, but they're gonna hit food trucks to starve the base. I need images of them at the perimeter fence when they leave."

"Are these guys going on a kill list?" asked Derrick.

"Grow up, mate," said Woody. "You should know this is about more than just killing people."

Woody had a way of making Derrick feel like a school kid but he never had the right thing to say at the right time. "I can do more than just take their photo, what do you need?"

"Ha ha, fuck off Derrick! Just make sure you are part of the patrol tomorrow morning at 0300. We think there's going to be a strike."

Striking food trucks was a common technique used by the Militia and Derrick wanted to highlight their duplicity to the world. The Islamic State got the blame for the strikes, which in turn increased the popularity of the Militia to provide security. It also deepened the distrust between the U.S. and Iraqi governments as protections for the Coalition degraded. Derrick thought he understood the situation and mission, and went to his room to sleep.

"You look shit," said the Russian when Derrick opened the door. "You should get some proper sleep."

"Don't you ever leave our room?" replied Derrick with a tired smile. "I didn't realise an intel deployment meant searching the internet from your bed…"

"Shhh baby, you talk shit, and you need your sleep. You know I work day-shift."

Derrick dropped his rifle, took off his pistol belt and then slumped in his chair.

"The threat to Coalition Forces has risen," said the Russian. "Insider attacks are now likely. Just make sure you're behind the rifle when it's fired … It'll be safer for you."

"Ha, thanks for the intel, mate," said Derrick as his eyes rolled to the back of his head and sleep consumed him.

At 2am, Derrick woke with a stiff neck, sitting slumped in his chair. With his alarm still buzzing he put his pistol belt back on, grabbed his rifle and started walking to the Operations Centre. A security patrol in a protected mobility vehicle stopped in front him and the Patrol Commander opened his door.

"Derrick, we just got a call from Akil to pick you up."

Akil? Where the fuck's he been? Derrick jumped in the vehicle and the Patrol Commander threw him an energy drink.

"Get that down ya! This could be a long one." The vehicle drove to the edge of the Green Zone and up an embankment to get eyes on Route Tampa.

"This is as far as we can go," said the Patrol Commander. The protected mobility vehicle hid behind a T-Wall, and Derrick poked his head through the hatch. He saw two white utility vehicles called 'technicals' outside the northern gate, both affixed with .50 Calibre machine guns to their trays. The moon lit the vehicles nicely, but Derrick's camera shutter speed was too slow, and the first image he took was blurry and out of focus.

"We have about a minute before they send up a drone," said the Patrol Commander.

"Just a second," said Derrick as he saw two men get out of the vehicle and open a suitcase. Red and green lights flashed from the ground. "Shit, it's a drone!" he yelled.

One of the diggers took his weapon and aimed from the back hatch. The drone killer looked like a rifle, but it cut the communications from the UAV to the controller.

"Hurry up mate," said the digger. "I can't hold this all night."

The distant Militiamen jabbered at each other as they wondered why the drone was not working, and one looked up and toward Derrick's position. Going stiff, he focused right where Derrick was. Cursing under his breath, Derrick hoped that they hadn't noticed any glints of light reflecting from his lens. No such luck. The two men deliberately aimed their AK-47s.

Derrick saw a flash from one of the muzzles and a round sailed over his head. "Contact fucken front," he yelled.

"Base Control this is ANZAC 20 we are in contact at North Gate. I say again, we are in contact at North Gate," radioed the Patrol Commander.

"ANZAC 20 this is Base Control, withdraw to a safe location and wait out for further instructions. Over."

"Time to go, Derrick. Get your shot and drop the hatch."

Derrick looked through his lens and got the picture. "Let's go!"

The Patrol Commander put his foot down and they withdrew to a safe distance and waited. "Base Control, have you got anything airborne?" he radioed again.

"Nothing ANZAC 20, drop Derrick at headquarters, and then keep eyes on the North Gate. Don't let anything through tonight."

The patrol took Derrick to headquarters, where he transferred the imagery to the thumb drive for Woody. He was too tired to think about the near-death experience he just had, and walked back to his room craning his neck around looking for falling rockets.

The next morning, Derrick opened his door and found Akil sitting outside his room slurping tea and reading a local newspaper.

"Have you read the news?" said Akil still glued to the pages. "Islamic State members killed near Tarmiyah."

Derrick walked out of his room and Akil handed him the local newspaper. "Well look at that, my photo made the front page," said Derrick with a smile.

"Have you had breakfast? The delivery truck made it to base, and there's lots of fresh food this morning," said Akil with a laugh.

They went to the dining facility and Derrick hammed up the night before. "The rounds were whizzing over my head Akil, you should have been there ..."

After breakfast, smoke had drifted over the camp and Derrick noticed Akil becoming agitated. "What's the matter?"

"They're burning rubber," Akil replied, distaste all over his face. "Not the Civilian contractors, this is the Militia. They'd be stupid to hit the base because they know the U.S. would strike back," muttered Akil. "But they can attack in small, mean ways."

Smoke hugged the ground, and the base went on high alert. Derrick's chest began to hurt from breathing shallowly, and his eyes felt all gritty and scratchy. He couldn't eat his lunch with the foul stench clinging to his nose and mouth, and his stomach rolled uneasily.

"The Militia is making things uncomfortable," said the Coalition Commander at an update brief that afternoon. "Contractors can't get to work; their base access passes have been revoked. Sewage is overflowing and the facilities manager is withholding water. The camp is being held to ransom."

The Commander prepared Derrick and his colleagues for an attack on the base and warned them to stay alert until the strike window had passed. Smoke was still thick in the air when Derrick watched the sun go down and smoked a cigarette in his bunker.

When he woke the following morning, he found the Russian panting in the foetal position moaning that he couldn't breathe. Their room stunk of soot and Derrick had a sore throat. "I'll check the smoke outside," said Derrick.

It was still dark but when he opened the front door, but it was the cold he noticed, not the smell of the smoke. Snow had blanketed the ground and flakes were twinkling in the dark sky. "It's snowing!" he shouted.

It hadn't snowed in Baghdad for eight years and Camp Cooke looked like a magical fortress. Derrick picked up his camera and ran to headquarters to capture the moment. Coalition flags gently waved in the breeze and yesterday's smoke had turned the sky to a beautiful shade of burnt purple. *Let's see if this makes the paper,* thought Derrick capturing the war zone's momentary beauty.

With mud all over his uniform and boots, Derrick walked into his office stinking of cigarettes and tyre smoke. The Coalition Commander was in early and chatting with Akil in the hallway when he walked through the door.

"Morning, Derrick," said the Coalition Commander. "Akil needs to go to the Australian Embassy in Baghdad — can you and Killer go as well?"

"Sure, Sir, but I go on leave to Australia in a couple of days?"

"Good, we'll see you back here tomorrow," said the Commander who then walked into his office and closed the door.

"The Militia has kidnapped a Coalition soldier," said Akil.

"Because two of their soldiers got whacked the other night?" asked Derrick but Akil didn't acknowledge his question.

"Let's find Killer," said Akil.

They found Killer smoking a cigarette for breakfast outside her accommodation.

"Were going to Baghdad for the night," said Derrick. "So, grab a day-bag and your camera kit."

A Black Hawk was waiting at the flight line to take Akil, Derrick and Killer to Baghdad. By the time they got there, the snow had melted and the ancient city glistened in the morning sun. Akil pointed out the old Baath Party headquarters, the Crossed Swords of Victory Arch, and he gave them a quick tour of Forward Operating Base Union III.

"Who was Saddam again?" asked Killer. "I don't want y'all to think I'm stupid, but we don't get taught that no more. We just know the Islamic State are terrorists."

"How do you not know these things?" asked Akil.

"He was the President, right? With the WMDs?" replied Killer.

Almost angry, but grateful for the opportunity to educate, Akil gave Killer a rundown of the Iran – Iraq war and Operations Desert Storm, Iraqi Freedom and Inherent Resolve.

"My country has been at war longer than you have been alive," said Akil. "I have a job for you — I want you to shoot a photographic essay of the Baghdad Green Zone. You'll be safe, but be back by dark, or I'll come to find you." Akil handed Killer a list of spots to shoot and gave her an access pass for the base and her room.

"Put on civilian clothes ... And don't draw attention to yourself," shouted Derrick, as Killer ran off grinning with her new assignment.

"Woody will follow her — we're expecting Militia to be in those locations, and we need her images for evidence," said Akil.

"It's starting to make sense," said Derrick. "We photograph the Militia and they wind up dead."

"You provide evidence — that is all Derrick," said Akil staring into Derrick's eyes.

A familiar black SUV gently pulled up next to them and the window wound down.

"You look and smell terrible! Let's get you cleaned up," said Emily.

CHAPTER 21

Like planting IEDs, the Militia used kidnap for ransom to gain political advantage, and though the Coalition suspected the Militia colluded with the Iraq Army, they needed the evidence.

"You don't think Killer's gonna capture collusion in the Green Zone, do you?" Asked Derrick as they waited for her at her accommodation pod that afternoon.

"I fully expect the Militia to be that brazen, yes."

The late sun cast a long shadow as Killer walked back to her accommodation and Derrick noticed the pavement change colour before she emerged around a corner.

"I don't know why y'all got me to shoot these places," said Killer handing over her memory card. "Just a bunch of Iraqi dudes having lunch."

"A cultural tour," said Akil, with a deadpan face that made Derrick want to laugh. "I'll have a look at your shots and tell you what I think tomorrow."

"I'm staying at the Embassy tonight," said Derrick. "But text me if you have any problems, you know where the dining facility is right?"

"I know everything about this base now — I'll be fine Mr fancy pants," said Killer with a strong southern drawl.

"Good job today … I'll see you in the morning," said Derrick who walked back to the flightline where the Black SUV was waiting.

"See you in the morning," said Akil opening the door for Derrick to get in.

"Where are you going? I know, I know, you have work to do. See you in the morning, said Derrick."

On arrival at the Australian Embassy security guards took Derrick's rifle and pistol and ushered him into a quaint private room overlooking a beautiful courtyard illuminated by the full moon. Some loafers, a pair of chinos and a collared shirt sat neatly on one of the chairs and a single cold beer stood on the table. Derrick had a quick shower and changed before taking a swig of beer just as Emily walked in.

"Wow," said Derrick who couldn't help but stare at Emily in a long elegant black dress. "You look stunning."

"It's nice to see you out of uniform and freshened up too Derrick. Dinner won't be long; you don't mind if I join you?"

"Not at all ..."

They both sat down and Emily asked about his aspirations, and he got to know a little more about hers, until his curiosity about Akil got the better of him.

"What's Akil going to do if he finds the Militia colluding with the Iraq Army in Killer's images?" he asked, piqued that he didn't fully understand what was going on.

"That's for Coalition Headquarters to decide," said Emily before changing the subject. "I hear you're going on leave … Going to catch up with Charlie?" said Emily with a surprising sneer of distaste on her face.

Caught off-guard by Emily's comment Derrick struggled to find the right words.

"I don't know what I'm doing with Charlie. We're on, then off and I'm not sure where it's headed."

"Have you told her that?" asked Emily.

"Are you jealous?" said Derrick with a cheeky smile as he rested his right hand on her left forearm.

"It's probably best not to touch a diplomat in an Australian Embassy Derrick," said Emily and Derrick gently pulled back his hand. Emily the took his hand with hers and pulled him in to whisper in his ear.

"You might want to let her know, it's probably not going to work out."

The next morning, Woody dropped Derrick at the flight line where Akil and Killer were waiting.

"Good night?" asked Akil who then handed Derrick a newspaper. The headline read 'Iraq Army to the Rescue – Islamic State's failed kidnapping'.

"Militia caught with their pants down?" asked Derrick.

"Brigadier Khalil was very embarrassed one of his officers worked with the Militia to kidnap a Coalition soldier," said Akil. "The officer's since been replaced and the new base Facilities Officer will restore utilities and provide food to the camp again."

"Do you mean he was killed?"

"It's one thing to work with the Militia; it's another to embarrass the Iraq Army. We worked to protect to the reputation of our partner," said Akil who quickly turned the conversation back to Derrick. "I hear you had dinner with Emily ..."

Jeezus, these bastards know everything ...

The Coalition Commander was waiting for them when Derrick, Akil and Killer flew back from Baghdad.

"Good job in Baghdad," said the Commander.

Derrick suppressed a laugh when Killer looked confused but smiled politely.

"Derrick, how long are you back in Australia for?"

"A couple of weeks, Sir," Derrick replied.

"Let's hope it's a quiet couple of weeks then. We have bought a little time, but I suspect that won't last long. Just make sure you're prepared to come back at a minute's notice." The Commander walked away and Akil followed.

"I don't know what just happened, but I'm going back to my room," said Killer. "I'll see you when you're back." She walked off the flight line, leaving Derrick wondering if going home was the right thing to do.

I'll be back in a couple of weeks, and I need to figure things out with Charlie.

Back in his room, Derrick was surprised to see that the Russian was at work and not in bed. He packed a bag and that evening was high over the Arabian Gulf, watching lights from oil tankers twinkle below. A quarter of the world's oil supply stood still between two U.S. carrier fleets and Iran, and he felt like an insignificant pawn in a never ending geo-political battle.

After a three-hour flight from Baghdad, Derrick reached Camp Hollow, an Australian staging base in a non-descript part of the Middle East. He'd organised the time off to spend with Charlie, but the more he thought about home, the more his mind drifted back to Emily and Iraq.

In between theatre exit briefs, Derrick phoned Charlie, trying to look forward to the break.

"Hey, how's the summer of bushfires going?" asked Derrick.

"Where the hell are you, Derrick?" barked Charlie. "What the fuck have you been doing? Have you forgotten I'm still your girlfriend?"

Derrick looked at his phone and sighed. "Charlie, I'm sorry but I think our relationship's done."

"You've been fucking gone for months …"

"It was nice knowing you Charlie … but goodbye." He hung up and knew he would never see or hear from Charlie again.

Derrick flew back to Canberra and fell into a spiral of self-loathing. His tolerance for normal society had reached an all-time low and a creeping barrage of texts … *Answer your phone and talk to me* … from unknown numbers and social media accounts, kept him locked in a cycle of despair.

Just fuck off Charlie ...

As he lit yet another cigarette, wishing he'd never left Iraq, a text from Bulldog made it through the onslaught.

Derrick, I heard you're in town?

How did you know?

That Foreign Affairs lady from Sri Lanka got in touch ... told me to look after you. You alright?

Yeah mate — Just been hanging about at home after telling Charlie we're over. Keen for a beer?

Derrick ordered a cab and stood in the cool of the evening outside his apartment.

"Where are you going, Sir?" said the driver when he arrived.

"To the shops, and then on to O'Reilly's Pub," said Derrick who sat in the front seat next to him. The cab stopped at the local shops and Derrick returned with cigarettes in his pocket. "Thanks mate," he said when he got back in the car.

"Sir, we will have to start the fare again," said the driver.

"Why? This was a planned stop."

"I didn't think you were coming back," said the driver.

"So, you think you can charge me twice for the same fucking trip," yelled Derrick at the top of his voice. "You're a fucking thief and I'm reporting you," he said as he got out and slammed the door. By the time he'd walked the twenty minutes to meet Bulldog he'd cooled off, but he was still in a foul mood.

"Hey man," said Bulldog wrapping his arms around him in a brotherly hug. "I got you a beer — have you seen the projections for this new flu virus?"

"Flu ..." said Derrick, momentarily disarmed by Bulldog's embrace.

They sat down and Bulldog showed him a chart that predicted a total economic collapse of Western powers and the death of millions. "Take your money out of the stock market now, they reckon. What's going on in Iraq?"

"Mate it's a bloodbath over there and there's no way some sniffle is going to stop what's coming to Iran," said Derrick, laughing arrogantly.

"Dude, you're getting fed wrong information … You'll be lucky to get back home when this shit kicks off … trust me," said Bulldog.

For the next ten minutes and in a stream of consciousness, Derrick began to unpack an intergenerational war with the West, where subjugated civilians got in the way of great power battles. Bulldog sat on receive, and tried his best to understand what Derrick was talking about, but it was all going straight over his head.

"Mate slow down, you're talking at a hundred miles per hour," interjected Bulldog when he had the chance.

"Sorry," said Derrick. "I feel like I've only done half the job over there and I can't switch off. I need to get back and help …" Derrick looked down at his phone and stood up. "I wish I could stay for another, but I need to get home and sort my shit out."

"I'm worried about you, man," said Bulldog bringing Derrick in for a hug. "When you're back let's do something to take your mind off work."

"For sure, and don't forget to stock up on toilet paper and tissues," said Derrick with a smile as he walked out.

Almost as soon as he got home, his phone started to vibrate.

We need you back, read Emily's text.

Okay, I'll leave tomorrow, replied Derrick.

Bulldog said you're a bit stressed?

154

Nah, I'm good, just keen to get back to work.

Good ... The U.S. think a strike on the Coalition is imminent. They're readying for war.

It felt like an age since Derrick was last in Baghdad, and as he boarded the charter flight back to Camp Hollow in the Middle East, he immediately felt wanted again. He scribbled thoughts in his notebook and read the local news.

'Militia embargo food', was the first headline Derrick read as he prepared to fly back into the country. The Militia was tightening their grip on Iraq and they had begun to control the flow of goods to and from the capital.

After little sleep on the 14 hour flight Derrick texted Emily.

I'm in Dubai.

We got hit last night ... Emily replied.

Jeezus, are you ok?

Five rockets landed a few metres from the Embassy, but no-one was killed.

I'm on a Herc in two days, Derrick texted back.

I hope you get back in ... Officials are turning planes around once they've landed.

What do you mean?

The U.S. told training forces to leave Iraq. The Militia is influencing Government.

Is the Coalition leaving Camp Cooke? asked Derrick.

Yes. I'll get you through customs if I can.

Derrick was still staring at his phone when Akil called.

"The Army is breaking," said Akil. "The Militia have bought Brigadier Khalil and he is working directly to them. The surrounding units are still friendly... but for how long?"

"I'm stuck here for the next two days," said Derrick. "Can I help?"

"Not until I tell you."

Akil sent Derrick some images and then rang again. "Send the images from an anonymous email to the Middle East desk at the BBC. Tell them you have a contact at the base that's just been hit by the Militia."

"What?" said Derrick.

"We're going to get hit … When we do, leak the images and the media will squeeze the Militia politically. When you get back here, we can finish the job." Akil hung up.

Finish the job. What does he mean? Confused, Derrick set up a fake email account, but felt incapacitated. The Militia was going to strike the base, but he couldn't tell anyone. He thought of his mates, the Russian, the Coalition Commander, and Killer. *They've been planning for a strike for months. They'll be okay, they're fucking pros.*

He felt sick and went to the gym to burn off the angst. He was dripping with sweat but couldn't stop looking at his phone. It was dark by the time he got back to his accommodation where he lit a cigarette in the moonlight.

Please don't get hit tonight …

Finish what job? he repeatedly asked himself before falling to sleep.

The call to prayer woke him early in the morning, and he looked at his phone. *Nothing.*

The flight line was a short walk from Camp Hollow and Derrick walked over to see if the Hercs had been allowed entry into Iraq.

"You on tomorrow's flight?" asked one of the crew who saw Derrick walk into the hangar.

"Yeah, I heard flights were being turned around."

"It's on mate, we're starting to pull people out of country. We'll get you back in, but you might not be there for long. Collect your rifle and body armour at 0530 and come back here."

Derrick left the hangar and was walking to breakfast when it dawned on him. "Fuck, the Militia's going to strike tonight ... They know we're pulling out!"

Derrick sent a message to Akil. *As soon as I see an 'incoming' alert I'm hitting send.*

It was twelve hours before Derrick got a reply, just as the call to prayer signalled the end of day.

You remember the strike window? read Akil's text. *Yep ...*

They were now in the strike window, and Derrick sat by himself and smoked anxiously. As he stared at his phone, the alert that he'd been waiting for flashed up on the screen.

Incoming - Incoming - Incoming, read the text from base ops.

"Shit! Are they actually getting hit?" Derrick whispered. He had read this message countless times before. Usually, indirect fire landed miles away from Camp. He wanted confirmation, from someone, anyone, but knew nobody would reply to his messages even if the alerts were false positives. He looked at the moon and prayed.

"Lord, if I get caught for this, I'm going to the Hague."

Militia strike Coalition in Iraq read his subject line; he attached the images of Militia leaders — and hit send.

Almost immediately, notifications on his phone began to ping, and news alerts began to detail the strike.

Helpless and shaking with panic Derrick went to bed and pulled a pillow over his head.

As the sun rose the next morning, he trawled through media sites to find his imagery. It was noticeably absent. He also tried to contact his mates in Camp Cooke, but it was clear they were in a communications blackout.

Three dead in strike on Coalition read the tabloids.

How do they get the information so quickly? thought Derrick.

At 5am, Derrick stood under a cold shower hoping to pull himself out of a bad dream. But when he couldn't, he walked to the hangar to collect his rifle and body armour.

"You're not going to Camp Cooke today, mate," said one of the air crew. "Rockets hit the runway."

Two Special Forces soldiers brushed past Derrick as he stood still and emotionless.

"Bad luck, mate," said one of them as they walked onto the waiting Hercules.

Sorry, I couldn't get you on, read a text from Emily a few moments later.

SF jumped straight on? he replied.

You're not SF and we can't blur the lines. BBC has reported a leak from Baghdad. Intel re the attack. Militia's under pressure and threatening war. We're trapped.

Derrick immediately felt sick and walked to a nearby bin to throw up. *Akil's going to get everyone killed and I helped him.* He scrolled through the rest of his messages. Some were from the Operations Centre and some from his mates saying they were okay. But Akil's message took his attention.

The media has applied the pressure we need. Standby.

Derrick saw red and didn't respond, he wanted to kill Akil. The secret he carried burned in his head and he felt like a traitor. Another sleepless night stole his energy and panic gripped his mind. Questions stacked up like bricks, but two key ones kept repeating: Who was Akil and what was he doing?

CHAPTER 22

At Camp Cooke, smoke rose from burning buildings and medical trauma teams still worked on the wounded from the previous night's strike. Multi-launch rocket systems fired over thirty rockets into Coalition facilities and the Militia had killed one British and two U.S. soldiers.

Battlefield Iraq – The War between the U.S. and Iran, read the news alert on Derrick's phone.

You see … read a message from Akil minutes later. *The media will shape public opinion. They will pressure Iranian factions in Government.*

Vision of crowds screaming 'Iran out of Iraq' from Tahrir Square in Baghdad spread on social media and Derrick was glued to his phone's news feed.

Clever thought Derrick as he watched on from Camp Hollow. *Akil manipulated me and the media to change state behaviour. But at what cost? Three of our mates are dead. Fuck Akil.*

At lunch, Derrick was lost in his thoughts when Akil messaged again.

Smoke and fog have blanketed the camp.

It can't be another strike … thought Derrick.

Iraqis had massed outside Camp Cooke, and their videos were circulating on news feeds. "Fuck, they know a strike's imminent," yelled Derrick as he scrolled through the content.

Incoming – Incoming – Incoming, flashed up on his phone and he jumped up and yelled, "Faaaaaaark."

"What's going on, Sir?" asked a Watchkeeper sitting close to him.

"Camp Cooke's getting hit again. It's a daytime strike."

The Watchkeeper immediately stood up and ran from the dining facility to the joint operations room.

Derrick continued staring at his phone until he noticed a woman in a flying suit approaching at a brisk walk.

"Sir, your bags are on board our Herc and you're leaving in ten," said the woman.

"What? Camp Cooke's currently under attack!" said Derrick despondently.

"Dude, I've just been told to get you ready," said the woman. "Your passport's been stamped and your rifle and armour will meet you at the flight line." She then ushered him towards the hangar, where a familiar face greeted him on arrival.

"Put your armour on and grab your rifle," said Woody.

"Woody, what the fuck are you doing here?" asked Derrick.

"Only SF in and out of the country, mate, and I've got cargo. Somebody thinks you're worth killing."

Derrick walked inside the Herc and the ramp closed behind him. The red lights came on and they bumped through the clouds until the plane dropped from thirty thousand feet and landed in what felt like seconds. He was back in Iraq.

"See you soon," said Woody over his headset. The Herc's tail door dropped when they braked to an urgent stop, and Derrick walked out into Camp Cooke.

An old British warrior stood waiting to greet him as the Hercules powered back up and taxied away.

"Fucking Derrick, how the hell are ya?" yelled the warrior.

"More to the point, how are you?" shouted Derrick as the roar of the engines dulled.

"To be fair, it's been a bit fucking hairy, mate, a bit like the old days."

The old warrior then punched Derrick in the kidney, like he always did. "Good to see you, mate. Now get on the fucking bus. The boss wants to see you."

When Derrick arrived at headquarters, the staff ran around nervously, with any modicum of noise sending their hearts racing.

"Derrick … my office!" shouted the Commander having seen him just walk in.

When Derrick walked into the office, Akil stood next the Commander.

"Good to see you my friend," said Akil.

The blood drained from Derrick's face and he was white with rage, but the Commander's brisk voice didn't give him any time to wallow in his emotions.

"Sit down," snapped the Commander. "Politicians have accused Brigadier Khalil of orchestrating attacks on his own base and now the Militia think he's sloppy, and the government officials want him dead — he's backed into a corner and becoming more dangerous by the hour."

"The U.S. has told all training teams to get out of Iraq," said Akil. "They're planning to take on the Militia and the Coalition needs to get out of the way."

Derrick's gaze burned through Akil, but he knew he didn't have the full picture. He felt used and needed to make sense of the conflating narratives running wild in his brain. "So why did you get me back here?" he asked, hoping his next task would make more sense.

"Go with Akil to Brigadier Khalil and tell him we're leaving. You're to take his portrait and design a gift so we can present it to him … as a token of our lasting friendship."

Derrick walked out of the Commander's office and grabbed the camera from his gear. Then he walked outside Coalition Headquarters to where Akil was waiting, smoking.

"Do you want to kill me?" said Akil smugly, taking a long drag of his cigarette.

"Why would you think that?" asked Derrick, his anger returning.

"I see from your face that you still don't understand," said Akil calmly.

"Who the fuck are you? Does Emily know? Does Woody?"

Akil's dark brown eyes stared soulfully at Derrick. "You think I am Militia?"

"It was as though you begged the Militia to strike again," said Derrick, almost spitting with rage. "And it was me you manipulated to do your dirty work."

"Why did you come back to Iraq? To demonstrate your naivety … to save Emily?"

"You're going to get us all fucking killed in your war against Iran … and I'm fucking complicit," yelled Derrick.

A clerk sitting inside headquarters heard Derrick yelling and ran outside to see what was going on. Akil smiled warmly at the woman and with a wave signalled that there was no problem.

"Control your emotions," Akil muttered under his breath, and the woman returned inside.

"Fuck you," said Derrick. "Three people have died. Friends of ours."

"I'll walk you back to your room," said Akil quietly. "We can take a car from there."

"Why didn't you give me the full story?" said Derrick, still seething. "Anyone could have sent those images, why me?"

"We trust you, Derrick … Emily, Woody the Commander and I, and we need to show world the Militia is strangling Iraq."

As they weaved through the T-walls and got closer to the accommodation pods Akil pulled Derrick a little closer with his arm. "Your neighbours have moved out," said Akil. "A 107 landed on their roof while they were at Ali's getting haircuts."

The bombed out remains of his neighbour's accommodation greeted Derrick with the sobering reality of his situation.

Akil drove Derrick outside the Camp Cooke Green Zone to Brigadier Khalil, who was suspicious yet accommodating when they arrived.

"Akil, Derrick, you've driven here alone … without a security detail," said the Brigadier. "This must be serious or very foolish considering the current circumstance."

"Sayidi, I have news," said Akil standing outside the headquarters. "The Coalition has been replaced by the Americans; they are already here."

Brigadier Khalil didn't react to Akil's statement but looked at Derrick with a quizzical stare. "Why did you come to tell me that? Derrick?"

"Sayidi, we want to thank you for your support and protection," replied Derrick glibly, keeping his face neutral. "We all worked together to get rid of the Islamic State. I'd like to take your portrait so we can present you with a gift on our departure."

"Take my portrait? Of course you can take my picture, Derrick. It would be my pleasure. The Coalition did help us to rid Iraq of the devil. And now the U.S. has moved back in … From one devil to the next."

Brigadier Khalil stood proudly while Derrick lined him up. He breathed out slowly taking a sight picture and pulled the trigger of his camera to capture history.

"I'll call you soon, Sayidi, so the Coalition can farewell you properly," said Akil, before the Brigadier walked back inside his headquarters.

"Let's go," said Akil, turning to Derrick with a satisfied look.

On their way back to the Green Zone, the stray dogs howled and burning rubbish infused the air. Akil drove through the tank graveyard where the remnants of the Iran – Iraq war slowly rusted into the earth and Derrick captured the history through his lens.

When Derrick arrived back at Coalition headquarters he walked into his office and called out for Killer.

"Killer's been moved on, Sir," said the clerk at the front desk.

"What?"

"She left Iraq this morning."

"This morning!" shouted Derrick.

"You were arguing outside with Akil when they told her she was leaving."

"Fuck!" yelled Derrick. "I'm such a selfish prick — so worried about myself, I didn't get to say goodbye."

"Sorry, Sir. I came out to tell you, but Akil shooed me back inside."

Derrick was feeling depressed and emotional when the Commander walked into his office.

"Where's the portrait?" asked the Commander.

"I just took the photos, Sir, I'll start designing something now," said Derrick.

"Okay," said the Commander, who was beginning to look worse for wear. "I need Brigadier Khalil to know that we really appreciate his help — we would have fared a lot worse if it weren't for him."

"Got it, Sir," said Derrick, and he put his feelings aside to get to work. He worked through the night to tell the story of their shared successes in a single image.

In the morning, the image was framed with an Arabian scimitar sword, and looked fit to be presented to Arabian royalty.

"Good work, Derrick," said the Commander when he walked in. He took the gift and read the inscription on the scimitar. "Brothers in Arms – Brothers for Life. Nice touch. We present these tomorrow … Go and get some sleep, you look sick."

Derrick walked back to his accommodation and when he opened the door, he found that Killer had left a farewell gift on the table. *Thanks for the education*, read the card. It sat on top of a southern American-style cowboy hat with a cinnamon candy 'Tootsie Rolls'.

"I was told not to eat these, but they're very tasty," said the Russian who was lying in bed again. "Where have you been, baby? I didn't see you yesterday."

"I need to sleep mate, I'll explain later," said Derrick.

"Go to sleep, baby … But keep your helmet and amour close."

Derrick put his mattress under the bed frame and draped his body armour over the top. Putting on his helmet, he drifted off to sleep with visons of explosions, sirens, and Emily swirling through his mind. He woke to the base alert system at 7pm; it was pitch black and he hadn't his left bed all day.

"Are we heading to bunkers?" asked Derrick.

"Keep down," said the Russian, who also hadn't left the room.

Derrick presumed the loud thuds outside were rockets landing close by and he reached for his body armour and put it on. After a few minutes of silence, they heard movement and scurrying outside. Derrick and the Russian emerged from their room and ran to the bunker, where Akil was standing at the entrance.

"Go back and get your rifle, you'll need it," said Akil.

The Russian's car was parked next to the bunker and he walked past Akil, got in and drove away toward the Operations Centre.

"Shit! He's driving off without us," said Derrick.

"Let's walk," said Akil calmly. "If you get hit, it won't matter if you're walking or in a car. The Commander wants all headquarters staff in place to assist the injured, and to take a rollcall of everyone on base in the event of another strike."

Thunder clouds had built during the evening and lightning flickered across the sky as they walked to headquarters. A Coalition Major was pacing the operations room floor when they arrived, and he looked straight at Derrick as he walked through the door.

"Calm and collected, keep calm and collected," the Major muttered ominously before the operations Watchkeeper radioed through to break the awkward stare.

"No reports of rockets landing on base — rest in place until further instruction," said the Watchkeeper.

The headquarters staff slept on floors and tables until the Commander told them to stand down at 2am. "Check the bunkers to make sure they got the message," said the Commander as they made their way out.

On the way back to his room, Derrick poked his head into a bunker that was still packed full of people. "Y'all can go back to your rooms now," said Derrick.

"No fucking way, Sir," replied a U.S. soldier. "We lost two of our friends who were lying in their beds, and we seen a bunker take a direct hit where everyone survived. We ain't going anywhere."

Derrick couldn't argue with the soldier's logic, and after checking in on a few more bunkers that were empty, he finally walked into his room at 3am.

Dear Jesus, Allah and Buddha please let the Militia sleep tonight he prayed.

CHAPTER 23

Training staff and non-essential personnel departed Iraq in droves after the most recent strikes, but the threat also bolstered the U.S. presence with C-17s filled with heavily armed troops arriving regularly to take over base control. Derrick noticed the soldiers' apprehension.

"Glad you're on Ops?" Derrick asked a young soldier who had just arrived and was standing outside headquarters.

"Man, we were supposed to be chilling in Cuba," said the soldier from Nashville. "We were going to Guantanamo, and then this happened. And y'all are bailing — we ain't ready for this shit."

A strong wind started to swirl around camp and a reconnaissance balloon high in the sky began to shake wildly — it then snapped from its tether.

"Oh shit," said Derrick, pointing towards the sky. "We better tell the guys in the operations room old blimpy boy has taken the day off."

"Goddamn," said the young soldier, who followed Derrick inside headquarters.

They ran into the operations room to see the balloon's camera operator watching the vision distort on his screen … then cut to black when the communication link broke.

"Mother fucker, the balloon's sailing to Iran," shouted the operator. "Call the Iraqis and get the air weapons team on station; we need to track this thing."

The balloon was an early warning platform meant to inform operations staff of an impending attack, but it was commonly down because of wind and storms. When it was up the Militia tended to lay low. Derrick knew they needed that balloon back in the air urgently.

Two Apache gunships took off from the flight line to monitor the balloon's trajectory and to make sure the Militia knew not to touch it when it landed.

The balloon floated 20 kilometres north of Camp Cooke, where it gently landed in a field of wheat.

"Angel overwatch has landed," radioed in one of the Apaches. This was also the trigger for the quick reaction force to deploy and a Black Hawk on station moved in. It hovered a few metres above the field and an infantry section rappelled down to secure the site.

"The Iraqis will be on scene in 20 Mics," a Battle Captain radioed through to the team on the ground.

"Woooah," yelled the new camera operator watching on. The soldier from Nashville stared at Derrick, who was watching a real time feed from a Predator UAV.

"So not ready for this," said the soldier.

Once the excitement died down Derrick walked outside, and found Akil stood next to a firepit burning like the midday sun. "Where is everyone?" asked Derrick.

"The Commander put most of the headquarters' staff on a Hercules this morning," said Akil.

"Everyone's fucking left?" shouted Derrick, but a car horn drowned out his scream. The car screeched to a stop in front of him.

"Derrick, get in Akil's car and follow the convoy," yelled the Commander from the passenger side of an up-armoured black pick-up.

Akil pointed to his light-skinned SUV parked outside headquarters, and they ran to make sure they joined the convoy.

"Fuck, what now?" asked Derrick.

"We're going to present the gifts you helped make, then you are also leaving — tomorrow."

"Jesus Akil, why is it always you that tells me this shit?"

"It's also Emily's birthday and I sent her a gift from you."

"You have to be kidding!" said Derrick.

"She likes honey, and I put a jar in her room with a note from you."

"You can't be serious; she'll think I'm fucking crazy."

Akil looked over and smiled. "Derrick, relax man, you're wound so tight. I didn't do anything."

"Arrrrgh!" shouted Derrick as they bumped through lanes of T-walls and passed out through the Green Zone.

"Everyone will be here, our partners and friends … and the Militia that conducted the attacks too.

"You have to be kidding!" blurted Derrick.

"Jealousy will rage when we present the gifts to our friends — status is everything and our praise will splinter the factions."

The convoy screeched to a halt and security cleared the area. Derrick then followed Akil and the Commander to Brigade Headquarters where the Iraqi Army had arranged a small ceremony.

The Coalition Commander heaped praise on his Iraqi counterparts like theatre, but the strain was evident in his eyes. The carefully crafted gifts and choreographed performance played to their host's egos and immediately garnered results.

Derrick looked through his camera at expressions of friendship and contempt as the gifts divided the ceremony. When Brigadier Khalil spoke warmly of the Coalition and their united efforts the Militia screamed in Arabic and stormed out. Akil already had the shots he needed when reports of indirect fire came in over the radio.

"Thank you for all that you have done to protect our forces for the past five years," said the Coalition Commander.

"You're always welcome in Iraq," replied the Brigadier.

The Coalition Commander and the Brigadier shared a quiet word, then the convoy left for Camp Cooke.

Late that evening, the U.S. and Coalition marked a transfer of authority to command the remaining personnel at Camp Cooke and the incoming Commanding Officer said some words.

"We're bolstering this base with firepower," said the CO. "We're thankful to the Coalition for the handover, but the base is our responsibility now. We're now in Iraq, not Cuba. But this is what you've trained for, so trust in your training and be good at your jobs. We hold God close to our hearts in the American south, so please join us in prayer."

The CO led the religious in prayer and that was it, the transfer was complete.

Akil moved over to Derrick and whispered in his ear. "I need to talk to you outside."

They walked outside and stood near the glowing fire pit that was burning everything from evacuation plans to heavy weapons and urban assault drills.

"The government has signed a deal with the Americans," said Akil. "Iraq will stop Iran from smuggling oil along the Shatt al-Arab river."

"What does that mean?" said Derrick.

"Iran is evading UN Sanctions," replied Akil. "They conduct illegal ship-to-ship transfers that support the regime. The U.S. wants it to stop, and I must help facilitate the UN inspectors. I'm leaving, now."

"What? You can't leave now!"

"Woody will take me back to Baghdad."

Derrick looked through the flames to see Woody staring at them. "There are way too many unanswered questions, Akil," said Derrick.

"I know, my friend … learn to relax, it will do you good." Akil smiled and opened his arms for a hug. "America is giving me citizenship soon," said Akil as he wiped the smoke from his eye and walked over to Woody.

Derrick stood staring at the flames. "Fuck!" he shouted at the top of his voice. His mind began to fill with all the questions he wanted to ask but he took a deep breath to stop the spiral of emotion. "Where the fuck is the Russian? I'm going to go home with him."

Derrick walked back to his room to find no-one there and the Russian's bags gone.

Shit, thought Derrick, *he must have left.* He checked next door — all the accommodation was empty. Derrick had never felt so lonely … he needed to find someone … anyone?

The sun was almost down, and the dogs were howling at the last of the dying light. He saw lights in the distance and noticed the Coalition Commander's pick-up driving slowly towards him.

"Are you alright?" asked the Commander.

"Where is everyone, Sir? I was just about to walk back to work," said Derrick.

"Don't bother, mate, the others have left. I sent them home on a Herc earlier."

"How did I miss that?" asked Derrick.

"Don't worry, you did good work today. Where's your camera?" said the Commander.

Derrick's heart sank. He hadn't seen his camera since the transfer of authority or Akil leaving. "Fuck, Sir, I'll race back to work and get it."

"Here you go," smiled the Commander and he threw it from the car window. "You won't need it again."

Derrick opened the memory card cover to see that the cards had been removed. "Fucking Akil," he said, and the Commander smiled.

"Grab a ration pack from the tray and I'll see you in the morning. We leave at 0600 from outside your bunker. And just an FYI, it might be worth sleeping in there tonight," the Commander laughed looking half delirious.

The Commander drove off and Derrick walked into his room and stared at the ceiling, worried at what might rain down. He lay restlessly thinking of home … then called his parents to calm his nerves.

"Hi Mum," said Derrick on hearing Kate's voice say hello.

"Derrick," shrieked Kate. "Hang on a minute and I'll get your father," and she ran off to fetch Geoff. It was early in the morning on the East Coast of Australia and the media hadn't reported on Iraq since Soleimani's death.

Derrick sat drumming his fingers until he heard her footsteps rushing back.

"Here he is," said Kate. "I've put you on speaker."

"Are the Americans at war with Iran yet?" said Geoff. "I thought after they killed Soleimani the Ayatollah would have hit back."

"They did," said Derrick. "They sent ballistic missiles into Iraq and hit bases to our north and south."

"Nothing was in the news?" said Geoff.

"Do they have a nice swimming pool over there, love?" asked Kate.

"Mum, I'm in a war zone."

"It's ever so hot here. The garden looks like death."

"Well, I hope the Americans get those bastards," said Geoff.

"We're leaving," said Derrick. "I'm coming home."

"The Iraqis are kicking you out?" asked Geoff.

"No, the Americans."

"The Americans should finish the job they started in the seventies," said Geoff. "Kate, you see, we should have moved to America when I told you to."

"Derrick, it was lovely talking to you," said Kate. "But we have to go, we're off to the local fair to help make tea and coffee."

"All right, have fun," said Derrick and he hung up. He grabbed his mattress and threw it into the bunker. Next, he grabbed his rifle, and then a text message made the phone in his pocket vibrate.

I'll meet you in Baghdad, read a text from Emily.

See you then, replied Derrick.

I must be going to Baghdad, thought Derrick, walking into the darkness of the bunker. His phone buzzed again.

And thanks for the honey, I love it xx.

Akil's a dead man, thought Derrick, smiling for the first time in days.

Shards of light lit each end of the bunker and he finally felt safe. He lay on his mattress and closed his eyes, the thought of seeing Emily comforted him and he fell to sleep.

In the early morning, he woke to the sound of rustling near his bags. He reached for his rifle and turned around to see the silhouette of a fox making a ghostly exit from the bunker. He remembered that he'd seen the fox when he first arrived at Camp Cooke. It was dawn, and he'd watched the fox weave through fog before the sun had fully risen. He raised his lens to take a shot, but the fox was cunning and disappeared into the mist.

Much like the Militia, he thought. Always present, but never in full view …

CHAPTER 24

Emily knew what time Derrick's flight from Camp Cooke was due into Baghdad, and it was late. There had been no reports of rocket strikes overnight, but she was concerned. She stood in the rain next to Woody, and her worry manifested to chatter. "Do the Militia know the Coalition is leaving?"

"Ma'am, we've had no reports of the Militia's intent to target Baghdad or Camp Cook in the last 24 hours," replied Woody who'd read the concern underlying Emily's question.

"I asked if they know we are leaving," Emily replied abruptly.

"They know the coalition has finished what they came to do, but they don't know when exactly they'll be out of the country."

"Why hasn't their plane landed? It's late ..." said Emily, frustrated.

Woody heard radio traffic through his earpiece and held a finger to his ear.

"Baghdad control tower this is Australian flight Kilo One, permission to land, over?"

"They're coming in now, Ma'am," said Woody.

Emily's anxiety eased for a second and she sent Derrick a text in the hope he might have reception on board. *When you get your passport stamped look for me*.

A Hercules landed with Australian markings — a kangaroo in a circle was everything that represented home for Emily.

With his rifle between his legs Derrick stared at the floor of the Hercules as they landed, his time in Iraq had ended too quickly and he needed closure. He also wanted to stay with Emily. Inside the plane a green light lit the fuselage, advising the occupants they could disembark.

"Follow the ground staff once you get out — get your passport stamped and get back on the plane," the aircrew yelled.

Derrick was the first to get off the aircraft and followed the ground staff to customs, where the same Iraqi official as when he first entered the country greeted him.

"Look at the camera," said the official, glaring at Derrick.

Derrick wondered where his picture might end up, but he smiled and the official clicked a button on his computer's mouse.

"Passport," demanded the official who sneered at him, then said "out" as he handed it back in what seemed a statement of disgust.

Derrick left customs to find the bathroom when Woody, who was dressed in chinos and a jacket, pulled him into a nook behind one of the T-walls.

"G'day mate," said Woody. Listen … you've made quite an impression on the boss, so wait here, and don't fuck off."

"Woody, the aircraft leaves in a few minutes," said Derrick.

"It'll go without you, if you don't stay there." Woody stared at Derrick with a calculating look before walking off behind a labyrinth of concrete and muddy lanes.

A soft hand reached around Derrick's waist, below his body armour, and he was drawn out of the rain into a dark bunker that ran parallel to the runway. He turned around and Emily's blue eyes immediately hypnotised him before she gently kissed him on the lips.

"Hi Derrick, there's so much I need to tell you," said Emily.

"Did we help?" asked Derrick.

"So much so."

"No one at home knows anything about what's happened here … nothing," said Derrick.

"They don't need to know," said Emily. "We protect them from this world, I'm sure you understand?"

"Come on," said Derrick. "The Government can't hide behind a one sentence press release … *All Australians are accounted for and safe* … my friends deserve more, and the dead deserve the people back home to know their story."

"Their story will be told but not now and not by us. We have a job to do."

"What job, what did we do?"

"We're not here to sell newspapers or to soothe your whimsical feelings." Emily's tone hardened and her eyes turned from blue to grey. "The forces at play here are much bigger than you and your lofty ideals … "I'm disappointed Derrick, when I marked you in Canberra as a junior Officer, I thought you had what it took to play this game …"

"That was you … This is a game to you?" said Derrick in disbelief.

"You're a wanted man now Derrick … influencing governments through the press … and I can't protect you if you won't see reason. No-one will care about your war-stories Derrick … no-one."

"You've been bought by the Government," said Derrick, fuming but simultaneously shaking.

"It wasn't supposed to end like this; this wasn't supposed to be goodbye." Emily looked into Derrick's eyes and paused for a second. "I'll let Woody see you off."

"At least I'm free and my hands clean," said Derrick in a moment of clarity.

Derrick felt Woody grab his body armour and press a cold and blunt object firmly into his spine.

"Hop on the flight mate, it's waiting for you."

Derrick walked out of the bunker and on to the tarmac where the aircraft had propellers turning. Aircrew marshalled him on board and he flew over the fields of Iraq for the last time, staring out at the bleak conditions.

A few hours later Derrick arrived back into Camp Hollow, where medical staff directed his movements. He was under orders to immediately fly back to Australia and to self-isolate at home for fourteen days. The virus Bulldog had spoken of only a couple of weeks ago was now killing people on a scale that saw terrorism relegated to the back pages of history.

The flight left Camp Hollow early the next morning, Derrick having had all but a couple hours of sleep. He arrived in Darwin 12 hours later, where a security guard swabbed him for explosives as he walked from the air bridge to the transit lounge bound for Canberra.

"Mate, you've just popped hot for explosives," said the guard. "If you've got shit on you tell me now, or you'll be charged."

Derrick looked at him with a blank stare.

"Alright, mate, I got to pat you down, so arms up and spread-em," said the guard who felt him up and down thoroughly.

"He's not talking, and I've found nothing," whispered the guard to his supervisor.

"Let him though … thanks for your service, mate," said the supervisor.

Derrick flew back to Canberra and caught a cab home to his cold, dark and silent apartment, where the door slammed closed behind him with a thud.

Well, that's it … I'm a prisoner to my thoughts … for two whole fucking weeks. He opened the fridge door to a case of beer waiting to welcome him home.

For days Derrick drowned the noise and anguish in his head. In a drunken stupor he took his marker pen and drew a stream of manic consciousness that began on his living room wall.

He drew images of chanting protesters in the streets and of his phone lit up with alerts. *Incoming – Incoming – Incoming ... Rest in place – Rest in place ...*

He drew smoke saturated sunsets, tyres burning, and the dark ghostly fox. Explosions, soldiers, helicopters, and the puppet master Akil came to life in his apartment.

Where the fuck is Akil? Where's Woody, the prick ... where's the Russian? Where's Emily? Fuck ...

Derrick rolled around in his bed, hating what he had become in the space of a few days. He forced himself to shave and shower and made a cup of strong, black tea.

God ... I need to make sense of this shit. He stared at the walls and paper strewn through his apartment.

Remembering that he'd turned his phone off, not wanting to talk to anyone, he reached for it and turned it back on, seeing that Kate had texted to welcome him home.

Glad you're home safe son. I just met Emily, who's lovely. She said you'll swing by before heading off again. See you soon love xx.

A loud knock at the door shook Derrick out of his confusion, and paper crackled and rustled as a note was slipped under the gap.

What the fuck! Derrick walked to the door and retrieved the note.

Pack your bags mate; I'll see you soon (W).

Derrick crushed the note in his palm and grinned with gritted teeth.